Also by Peter Carnavas

My Brother Ben
The Elephant

LEO and RALPH

Peter Carnavas

PUSHKIN CHILDREN'S

Pushkin Press
Somerset House, Strand
London WC2R 1LA

First publishing in the English language by
University of Queensland Press, Australia, in 2024.

This edition published under license from University of Queensland Press.

First published by Pushkin Press in 2025

1 3 5 7 9 8 6 4 2

ISBN 13: 978-1-78269-523-3

Offset by Tetragon, London
Printed and bound in the United Kingdom by Clays Ltd, Elcograf S.p.A.

www.pushkinpress.com

For my sister, Jo

PROLOGUE

Leo and Ralph lay on a blanket in the backyard, looking up at the night sky. It was dark but not too dark, as the glow from streetlights cast a soft haze across the neighbourhood. Only a few of the brightest stars poked through.

'Hey, Ralph.' Leo held a telescope to his eye. There was a crack on the lens. 'Which planet should we look for?'

His friend rattled a sigh, and his voice had a soft growl when he answered. 'Flumblebot.'

Leo smiled. Flumblebot was his favourite of all the planets they had invented. Home to a group of friendly aliens called Grimbles. They had two heads, smooth pear-shaped bodies and they spoke in backwards sentences.

'Okay, then.' Leo focused the cracked lens on a spare patch of the sky. 'If a Grimble from Flumblebot landed in this yard right now, what would you say?'

Ralph lay still. The reflection of a star twinkled in his eye. 'I'd say: snacks bring you did?'

Leo dropped the telescope and rolled over, laughing. Ralph always cracked him up like that. They had lain on this blanket, staring at the sky, hundreds of times. Dreamt of planets with funny names, imagined the creatures that lived there and the spaceships they might fly. If Mum didn't call out to Leo each night, he would probably never go inside. He'd stay out until morning, lost in those faraway worlds that no one else knew. No one – except Ralph.

They gazed up for a bit longer. Then, slowly, the night air cooled and something shifted in Leo. A cold feeling seeped into his feet and up through his body, the way a bad memory steps from shadow into light. The feeling came because Leo knew this was the last time he and Ralph would do this. The last time they would share this blanket on the grass, look through the telescope and talk about aliens. Tomorrow the truck would arrive and take all the taped-up boxes from the lounge room. All the furniture and everything from the garage. Then Leo would sit in the back of the car to wherever it was they were going, to start all over again. New town. New school. A new life without his best friend.

He sat up, crosslegged, with his chin on his fists. He couldn't imagine doing anything without Ralph. Before they met, he was like an asteroid, orbiting the other kids, not knowing what to do. As soon as Ralph arrived, school became less scary, the grown-ups stopped worrying and Leo had the friend of his dreams. He didn't want to go back to the way things were, especially in a place where he didn't know anyone.

The back door of the house squeaked open. Leo didn't turn round, but he knew it was Mum.

'Leo, love. It's nearly bedtime.' She waited, and he felt the whole world pause with her, as if that cold feeling had slithered across the grass and found her too. 'Two more minutes, okay?'

'Okay, Mum.'

The door clicked shut.

Ralph sat up. His voice was croaky. 'If a shooting star zoomed past right now, what would you wish for?'

'Easy,' said Leo. 'To stay right here.'

Ralph shook his head. 'Apart from that.'

'To take you with me.'

'Or that.'

Leo looked up at the blurry sky and tried to picture an alien ship floating down. Blinking lights, a soft swooshing sound, the strange shape of it getting bigger. Then the back door squeaked open again. Mum was there, waiting.

Leo faced his friend. He was hunched on the blanket, his hair was moon-grey and his wet eyes shone in the dark.

There was only one thing to wish for.

'To find another friend like you.'

They hugged for a long time. Ralph always gave the best hugs. Then they said goodbye the way they always did: backwards, like the Grimbles from Flumblebot.

'Tomorrow you see.'

'Tomorrow you see.'

It wasn't true. They wouldn't see each other tomorrow. But they couldn't bear to say goodbye any other way.

Leo let go of his friend and plodded up to the house. Before he went inside, he threw the telescope in the bin at the bottom of the stairs. He wouldn't need it anymore.

THE WHITE BALLOON

One day, when Leo was five, he saw a white balloon sweeping through the sky. It was a long way up and it bobbled as it streaked over his house, the way a bike shudders when it's going too fast. He ran around the yard to keep it in sight, and he wondered who had let it go. It was trailing a long ribbon, so it had probably escaped a birthday party, slipped from the hands of a kid like him. It flew further away, higher and higher, shrinking to a small white dot. As it grew smaller and then disappeared, he stopped thinking about where it had come from.

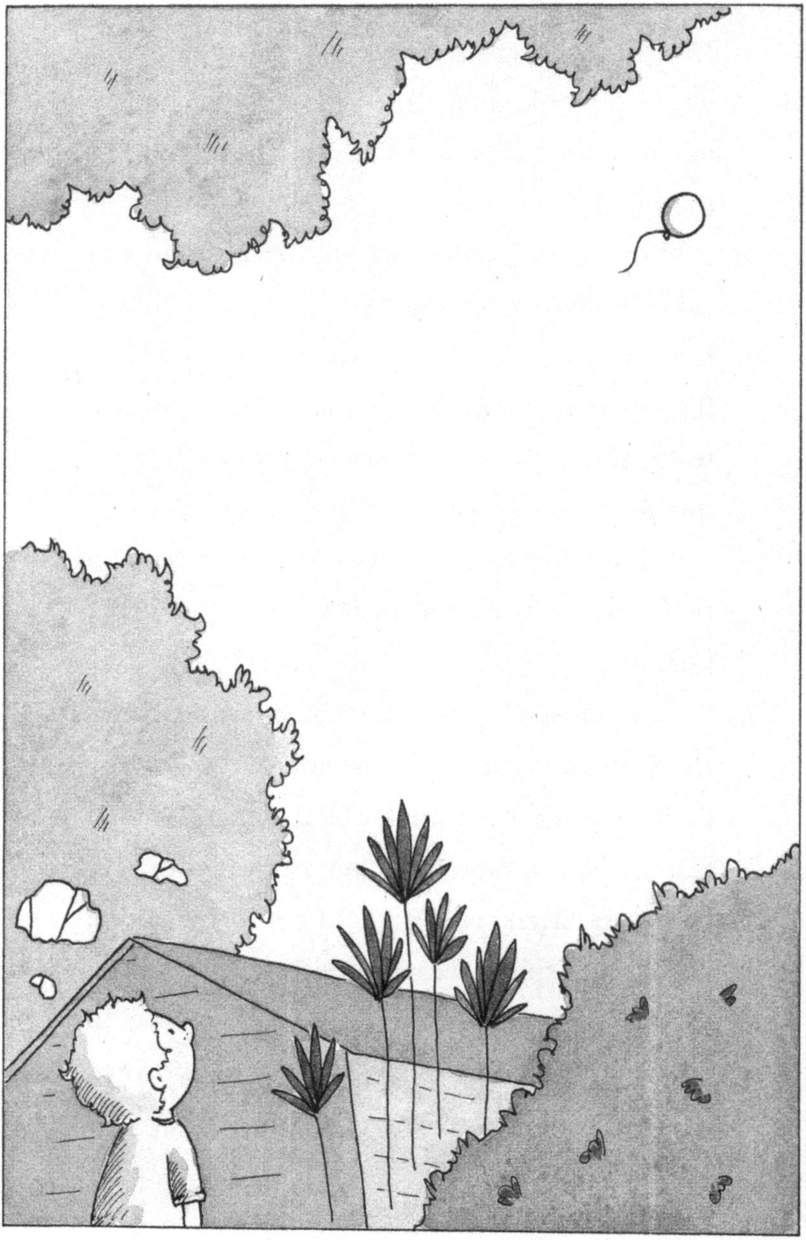

Instead, he wondered where it was going and where it would stop. If it kept floating higher, would it ever stop at all? The thought was almost too big to hold.

Lots of things felt too big because he was smaller than other children his age. His short legs could never keep up when they walked in lines at school, and he took longer than others to climb steps. He otherwise looked like an ordinary boy – pointy chin, freckled nose, a mop of sandy hair – but he never seemed to fit neatly into the jigsaw puzzle of other kids.

While they pushed tractors and spades through the sandpit, he wondered how many grains of sand were stuck to his palm. His Prep teacher had to repeat her questions because his eyes were often fixed on a corner of the room, watching a spider weave its web, or a raindrop wriggle down a window. He imagined faces in tree trunks, contemplated the life of an upturned beetle, and followed the epic journeys of ants as they carried their treasure from one end of a path to the other.

His head was filled with questions. Were his footsteps like earthquakes for tiny bugs in the grass? Why was an apple called an apple and cake called cake? What if everyone slept during the day and stayed awake at night?

He sometimes shared his thoughts with other kids, but he spoke too slowly for them to catch on.

'If … dogs could, er, talk, what would they …'

Why did his ideas come out like that? It was like the words had just woken up and were wandering round, trying to find each other. Mum said there was nothing wrong with taking time. Dad told him not to worry because the world needed to slow down. Either way, the other kids were baffled or bored. They didn't care for the size of his thoughts or the time it took to share them, and they butted in or walked away before he finished talking.

So Leo drifted to the fringes of playgrounds. He kept his ideas to himself, but they didn't stop growing, and his biggest thoughts came when he saw the white balloon that day. After it had blown over his yard, he thought about it all afternoon. That night, when he climbed into bed, the disappearing dot was still pulsing in his mind. He waited until his parents had put his little sister Peg to bed, then he asked Mum about it. She was a teacher, and he liked the way she explained things.

'How long will it float for?'

'Well …' She pulled the blanket up to his shoulders and flattened it over his chest. 'It'll float as long as there's air inside. A long time if the knot is tight.'

'Will it float forever?'

'I think it will come down one day.'

'Where?'

'Anywhere. In the branches of a tree. In someone's swimming pool.'

'What if the wind blows it higher?'

Mum put a finger to her chin. It was pointy like his, but her hair was dark like cocoa. 'A flock of geese will pop it if it gets too high.'

'Huh.' He almost laughed, but he was still full of wondering. He wanted to know more about the balloon and the sky and how big it all was. 'Mum.' His eyes were wide. 'Where does it end?'

She narrowed one eye. 'Where does what end?'

'The sky,' he said. 'Where does it end?'

She combed her fingers through his hair and held the back of his head in her hand. 'It doesn't end, Leo. It goes on forever.'

'Forever?'

She reached across him and opened the curtain just enough to see a piece of the starry night. 'Above the sky is space. It just keeps on going. And we don't know much more than that.'

He laughed this time. The whole sky – all that endless space – was suddenly inside him, filling his chest until he thought he might burst. It was the most exciting thing he had ever heard.

QUESTIONS

From that day on, Leo looked up. He thought about the colour of the sky and the coming and going of stars. He noticed the changing angle of the sun and when the moon hung around in the daytime. Mum could explain a lot about the sky. Dad helped too. He was freckled like Leo, but he mowed lawns all day, so the sun had turned his arms and legs the colour of golden syrup. In his spare hours, he drew pictures of animals, and in the afternoons, when he cooked dinner or read stories to Peg, he tried to answer Leo's questions.

'What's the sun made of?'

'Gas, buddy. It's a big ball of gas.'

'How does it stay in the air? Will it ever fall down?'

'I don't think so. Something to do with gravity.'

The biggest thoughts that Leo had were about deep space, the never-ending expanse of emptiness beyond the blue sky. He couldn't stop thinking about the wild impossibility of it all. But as his curiosity roamed further into the distant dark, his questions grew larger and the answers grew thin.

'How many planets are there?' He sat on the kitchen bench while his dad peeled potatoes in the sink. Peg was at the table, trotting the salt and pepper shakers around like they were best friends.

'Well, there are eight,' said Dad. 'There used to be nine. Pluto's not a planet anymore.'

'What happened?'

'Nothing, really. Someone just realised it wasn't big enough to be a planet.'

Leo swung his short legs. 'That's not fair.'

Dad grabbed another potato. 'But there are probably more we can't see. Way out in space. Just because you can't see something, doesn't mean it's not there.'

Leo's eyes twinkled. He liked that idea. 'How many more planets do you think there are?'

'No one knows. Millions, maybe.'

Leo felt the sky filling his chest again. His head swirled and his hands tingled. He wasn't sure what millions meant but he knew it was big. 'If there are millions of planets, then there must be other people out there.'

'Well, not people,' said Dad. 'Something else, maybe.'

'What, then?'

'Aliens, I guess.'

Leo repeated the word. 'Aliens.'

Dad put down the potato peeler. For a quiet moment, they both gazed out the kitchen window at the darkening sky. Leo didn't know what his dad was thinking, but his own thoughts shone as bright and clear as the first evening star. Something else was living out there and one day he would meet them. Just because you couldn't see something, didn't mean it wasn't there.

MUM'S WISH

One night, Leo heard Mum and Dad talking in the lounge room. He was in bed, but his door was open a bit. The television threw a hazy blue light on the walls and his parents spoke in quiet voices.

'Know what he asked me today?' Mum said. 'He wanted to know if we'd let an alien stay, if it landed in the backyard.'

'What did you say?'

'Sure, if it paid rent and cooked us dinner sometimes.'

They both laughed.

'Do you think … I don't know.' Mum's voice turned soft and serious. 'Do we need to worry?'

'About what?'

'All this space stuff.'

'Lots of people think about space.'

'But it's *all* he thinks about. And I'm worried he doesn't try with the other kids anymore.'

Dad let out a long, slow breath. 'They don't give him a chance. He tries to talk but, you know, his words …'

There was nothing for a while. Just the low mumble of the television.

'All his ideas, all his curious questions,' said Mum. 'I wish he had someone to share them with. I wish he had a friend.'

The television light flickered onto the walls for a while longer. Then his parents switched it off, went to bed, and Leo lay in the dark. He didn't sleep for a long time because he didn't know how to make his mum's wish come true.

DAD'S IDEA

The next morning, Leo finished his Rice Bubbles and rolled his coloured pencils onto the table. He opened to a fresh page in his scrapbook and started drawing. A round, furry shape with ten googly eyes. A long, green, spiky thing with wheels instead of legs. A fluffy cloud with lots of arms and a big pointy nose.

Dad stood close by, watching him. He smelt like sunscreen and he tucked his dirt-brown mowing shirt into his dirt-brown shorts.

Leo asked questions as he drew. 'How many yards do you mow?'

Dad laughed. 'Not enough.'

'Do you like mowing yards?'

'Someone's gotta do it. I'd rather be doing what you're doing. Drawing pictures.'

Leo swapped a green pencil for a blue. 'So why don't you draw pictures?'

Mum stuck her head in from the kitchen. 'Because if your dad drew pictures all day, we'd be living in a tent.' She poked out her tongue.

He stopped drawing. 'Why would we live in a tent?'

'Don't worry, bud.' Dad leant on the back of the chair and looked at the scribbly aliens. 'Does anyone at school like space stuff?'

Leo shook his head. He held his tongue out of the corner of his mouth as he drew.

Mum appeared, zipping up a lunchbox. 'Have you asked?' Then she wrapped her arms around him. 'You have all those space facts growing in your head. There must be someone at school who'd like to hear them.'

Leo chewed his pencil.

'Why don't you try today?' Dad pulled a wide-brimmed hat onto his head. 'Show someone your pictures. Tell them some things you know.' He patted Leo on the back. 'It'd be good to have a friend, buddy.'

Leo dropped his head. He knew what would happen if he tried to talk to the other kids. His words would sleepwalk, and everyone would butt in or walk away. It was easier to look out the window and up at the sky, to imagine a friend falling from space.

MORNING ACTIVITIES

The school day started on the colourful mat. Leo sat on the edge behind the other kids. Some of them tugged at their oversized uniforms, others keeled onto their backs and rolled around, unable to stay still. Leo sat straight, trying to keep his eyes ahead instead of staring at the sky outside the windows. Mrs Lloyd pointed to a weather chart, sang an alphabet song and read a book about a pig who sailed the world. A story about aliens skimming through space would have been better.

In Morning Activities everyone chose to

work at one of the stations around the room. There was a dress-up corner, a puppet theatre and tubs of building blocks. Leo sat at the construction table, a hexagonal desk with jars of buttons, beads, nuts and bolts, pipecleaners, pom poms and glue. He started with a big styrofoam ball and covered it with shiny beads and stickers. Then he remembered what his parents had said that morning and Mum's wish from the night before.

A skinny dark-haired girl sat on the other side of the table. He couldn't remember her name.

'Hey. Look at my, uh, planet.'

She didn't look up from the pipecleaner she was trying to cut in half.

'Did you know there are—'

'That's not a planet,' she snapped, without lifting her head. 'It's an ice cream that lost its cone.'

The next day, he went to the dress-up corner. He pulled a long stripy skirt up to his armpits, squished his feet into some flippers and clipped a pair of wobbly antennae to his head. Another boy was dressing up beside him. He was only a bit bigger than Leo and his name was Henry. Or Hugo. Probably Henry.

'Henry,' said Leo. 'Do I look like a—'

'Huh?' Henry had a beanie pulled down over his face and knocked over one of the dress-up tubs.

'An alien.' Leo pointed to his antennae, even though Henry couldn't see a thing. 'They, you know, they live in space.'

Henry ripped off his beanie and frowned. 'I'm James,' he said, and walked away.

On Friday, Leo sat at the drawing station. He used crayons to draw a round purple alien with a wonky smile and held it up to some other kids. A boy snatched the drawing, studied it, then drew an army tank rolling into the scene, its gun pointed at the alien.

That afternoon, the class gathered on the colourful mat. Leo was tired. He lay back and stared at some plastic stars stuck to the ceiling. There was another song and another book, but he just lay there, looking up. Right before home time, Mrs Lloyd announced her Star of the Day. It was the army tank kid.

THE ALBUM

Saturday morning sounds swirled through the house. The vacuum cleaner hummed. The washing machine tumbled and turned. Music swam through the open windows from a neighbour across the street. In the kitchen, Leo stirred a glass of chocolate milk, watching the whirlpool speed up and slow down. At the table behind him, Peg squished playdough into lumpy shapes.

Everyone was busy. That was good. Leo wanted to forget about school and hoped Mum and Dad would too. He joined Peg at the table, tore off a chunk of playdough and rolled it into a ball. When it was smooth and round, he added three eyes, a pair of horns and a line of spines across its back. He showed it to Peg.

'It's an alien,' she said.

He nodded. 'I'll call this one a … Gronk.'

He put it to the side and made some more. There was a cube-shaped creature with one eye, a lumpy yellow thing covered in pink spots, tiny round critters, long wobbly beasts, and one that looked human, only with two heads and an extra pair of arms.

He stood and admired his creations. Each alien was different, but they all looked friendly. Big smiles, wide eyes – he couldn't imagine any of them butting in or walking away.

'Are you going to keep them?' said Peg. 'I need more playdough.'

Leo ran into his room and found the polaroid camera he shared with her. He came back to the table, lined his aliens up in a row and took photos of them, one at a time. When the camera had printed the last picture, he squashed each doughy alien in his fists and gave the lot to Peg. Then he found a square notepad and stuck the photos on the pages. Underneath each picture, he wrote its alien name. *Gronk. Fump. Wozzle. Meeb.* Spelling didn't matter because it was all made up.

Peg was still prodding and poking the dough. She made blobby shapes and arranged them next to each other.

'What are they?' he said.

She placed a lumpy figure beside the others. 'Friends.'

He flipped through the pages of his alien album and smiled. 'Mine too.' Then he scrawled *Frends* on the front cover.

PEG

Peg was a year and a half younger than Leo. They looked alike with their pointy chins and sandy hair, but not much else was the same. She often rushed to the centre of the playground, spoke without a pause and, from the first day, had made friends at kindy. She wasn't loud, bossy or overly talkative – she was just a girl who other kids liked. But he didn't expect her – his just-turned-four sister – to give him advice over dinner that night.

Mum started it. As she dished fried rice into their bowls, she asked Leo about some of the kids in his class.

'What's little George like?'

He didn't know anything about George except that he wasn't little.

'What about Hunter – what does he do at playtime?'

'I don't know.'

'Let's think of some others. How about—' She stopped. 'Sorry. I sound like I'm teaching at school. It's just … I thought that—'

Peg interrupted. 'Why don't you join in a game?'

He held a spoonful of rice and looked at her. 'What?'

She shrugged. 'When I've got no one to play with, I just join in someone's game.'

'What sort of game?' said Mum.

'Tiggy. Hide-and-seek.' She looked deep into her bowl, as if more games were hiding there. 'My favourite one's Horsey.'

Dad gave her a serious look. 'Tell us about Horsey.'

She returned the expression. 'We pretend we're horses. That's all.' Then she burst out laughing.

Leo didn't laugh. He kept his head down. Gripped the spoon and scooped too much rice into his mouth. He tried to imagine himself joining in at playtime. He wouldn't know what to do. He wouldn't keep up. And there was no way he was going to play Horsey. The whole thing was a terrible idea.

'Well, I think it's a good idea,' said Mum.

'Me too.' Dad lifted his glass in a kind of salute. 'It's worth a try.'

PLAYGROUND

Leo wasn't sure where to start. He looked around for a game to join in and heard a thumping sound behind the Prep room. A group of kids were kicking a ball to each other on the small circle of grass. Leo stood to the side, watching. They yelled to each other in between kicks, but he couldn't work out any pattern or rules. Then the ball rolled towards him. He waited for it without moving and it bounced off his shin.

'Kick it!' someone yelled.

He had seen the others kick, so he stepped up to the ball and swung his leg. His foot missed, then landed on top of the ball. He wobbled over and fell to the ground. The others laughed as he lay there, wishing the sky would swallow him up. Someone else kicked the ball, the game carried on and he stumbled back to the classroom.

Next lunchtime, Leo stood in the playground in the shade of his big bucket hat. He looked like a tiny beach umbrella. The other kids swarmed past, under bridges, through tunnels, up and over climbing frames. They moved smoothly around him, like water rushing past an obstacle, and he wondered if they could see him. He didn't know their game, or how many games were taking place. Couldn't grasp the phrases they shouted at each other as they hung from bars and slid down poles.

He looked up. The sun was trapped behind a wall of cloud and the sky was whitish grey. He imagined the endless blanket of space beyond, the unknown planets and the aliens he wanted to meet.

'Oof!'

A tall boy bulldozed into him and Leo hit the ground. He wheezed a few raspy breaths and held his belly.

'Sorry!' The tall boy pulled him up by the wrist. 'Didn't see you.' He started to run off.

'Hey!' Leo yelled, still clutching his guts. 'How do you, you know, play …' But the boy was gone.

Leo brushed dirt off his palms and got his breath back. Then he stuck out a hand to stop a pigtailed girl who was sprinting past.

'What game are you pl—'

He couldn't finish because a red-haired boy on the climbing fort shouted, 'VOLCANO!' It must have been part of the game because a wave of squeals rang out across the playground and everyone bolted in different directions, including the pigtailed girl. Leo followed but couldn't keep up. He spun around, lost balance and was bumped over again. Kids thundered past like a herd of bulls. He ducked his head, crawled through the stampede and sat on a log, away from the crowd. His knees were scratched. His hands shook. The playground was a battlefield he didn't want to join.

At the end of the day, he lay on the colourful mat. Closed his eyes and imagined an alien ship hovering above the playground. He pictured a friendly Gronk jumping from the ship and landing beside him. They'd play a game that no one else knew, a game without volcanoes.

A sudden wave of applause startled him. He rubbed his eyes, sat up and remembered he was in the classroom. Kids all around him were cheering and clapping because Mrs Lloyd had awarded her Star of the Day: the red-haired boy from the climbing fort, the kid who'd yelled, 'VOLCANO!'

Leo still didn't know what it meant.

FAMILY DAY

Things got worse when Mum, Dad and Peg came to school for Family Day. It was an afternoon for the Preps to show off their schoolwork, but Leo dragged his feet like they were made of moon rock. He still hadn't made a friend. Mum's wish hadn't come true. And now they were at school, watching all the kids pretend he didn't exist.

Family Day started in the courtyard in the middle of the school. The class stood in line and sang a song about vegetables. Then everyone moved inside and looked at all the stories and paintings and cardboard buildings the students had made. Mum fussed over a picture Leo had drawn of an alien family, two big ones and two small.

'Which one's me? Ooh, that has to be Dad with three eyes.'

Finally, afternoon tea was set up in the courtyard and everyone was allowed free time on the playground. Leo stood next to one of the food tables, piling cream onto a pikelet. He waited for Mum and Dad to tell him to hurry up, to finish eating and go play. But they were already watching the action.

'Look at Peg on the monkey bars,' said Mum, licking cake icing off her fingers.

'How did she get up there by herself?' Dad sipped tea from a paper cup. 'Is she talking to someone?'

It was true. Peg was on the playground, swinging from bars, whizzing down slides and chatting to the other kids. All the things Leo was supposed to do.

Mum gave Dad a playful hit on the arm. 'We won't have to worry about *her* next year.'

Leo felt his eyes burn. Mum must have noticed because she bent down and held his hand. 'Oh, love. I'm sorry. I didn't mean—'

He pulled away and ran from the crowd to a spot under the office stairs. It was on the other side of the courtyard and hard to find, but with a good view of the sky. He looked up and saw the almost-full moon, hanging like a white balloon. He blinked until his eyes felt dry. Then he heard something that made his whole body – not just his feet – feel like a pile of moon rock.

'VOLCANO!'

It was Peg's voice. She wasn't just playing the game. She was in charge. Mrs Lloyd would probably name her the Star of the Day.

It was at that moment, under the office stairs, that Leo made an important decision.

He'd had enough of school. He wasn't coming back.

A LUMP OF WORRY

When Leo refused to put on his uniform, Mum and Dad didn't say much. Mum hugged him tight before she took Peg to kindy and went to work. Dad cancelled his mowing for the day and stayed home.

Leo changed out of his pyjamas sometime between breakfast and lunch – it didn't matter when things happened, without school bells and teachers around. He and Dad watched a television show about Jupiter. He already knew it was the biggest planet, but he didn't know it had over ninety moons. There must have been something living on them. They couldn't all be empty balls of rock.

Later, he joined Dad at the dining table with the bucket of playdough and the polaroid camera. The sun threw warm light on Leo's face. A plinky piano sounded from somewhere down the street. Inside his belly, a thick lump of worry washed away like a fistful of sand in the ocean. This was how life was supposed to be.

'I could do this all day.' Dad was drawing. He flicked neat pencil lines across a page, building them into a picture of a pug. Or was he drawing a cat? 'This would be great. Just stay home and draw. No more lawns. Of course, we'd have no money and we'd have to live in that tent Mum keeps talking about.'

Leo let out a soft laugh. He smooshed green and blue playdough together to make a wonky three-eyed alien. Then reached for the camera.

'So I'm going back to work tomorrow,' said Dad. He drew a bunch of sprouting whiskers – definitely a cat. 'And you have to go to school.'

The camera fell out of Leo's hands and hit the table. The sun hid behind a cloud and the lump of worry reformed in his gut. He gave up on his alien and went to his room.

ANIMALS

The next morning, Leo sat hunched between Mum and Dad as they talked with Mrs Lloyd. He tried to shrivel up so he was hardly there. The grown-ups talked about him as if he really was somewhere else.

'Leo's a bright boy,' said Mrs Lloyd with a lipsticky smile. 'He can read full sentences and can already count past a hundred. But I suppose you're here because …' She held her smile and sucked a breath through her teeth. 'Well, Leo doesn't join in with the other kids.'

He stopped listening. He caught grabs of

sentences and worried looks, but he had his eyes fixed on a pile of fluffy toys in the corner. There were teddy bears, a few dinosaurs and some farm animals. One of the toys was mostly buried under the others and all that poked out was a pair of stubby horns. For a moment, he imagined they belonged to an alien and he started to dream up a story. Maybe the alien had crash-landed on the school oval last night, sneaked into the Prep classroom and was now hiding among the toys, hoping no one would find it.

'What do you think, Leo?'

He blinked at Mrs Lloyd, who was waiting for an answer. He didn't know what to say, so he looked from Mum to Dad until one of them helped him out.

Mum pointed to a chart on the desk. There were pictures of coloured animals: a red bull, a white mouse, a blue penguin. 'Mrs Lloyd was just talking about these animals and how they show different feelings. There's an angry bull, a quiet mouse, and a sad penguin. Look over here, there's a brave lion and a cheeky puppy.'

Leo looked at the pictures. He didn't know what this had to do with anything.

'When you're at school,' said Dad, 'how do you feel? Which animal do you think you are?'

This was silly. He wasn't an animal and he didn't feel brave or cheeky or nervous or angry.

'Okay,' said Mrs Lloyd. 'Would you like to draw something?' She bustled across the room and came back with a tub of felt pens and a sheet of thick paper. 'Why don't you draw how you feel when you're at school.'

Leo uncapped a pen and drew a crowd of wobbly stick figures.

'Who's that?' said Mum.

'Other kids.'

Then he drew a blobby shape on the other side of the page. He gave it six eyes and four arms.

'And what's that?' said Dad.

Leo smiled. 'That's me.'

He dropped the pen in the tub. The grown-ups stared at the drawing. He pushed his chair back and went over to the fluffy toys. He plunged his hand into the pile and pulled out the toy with the stubby horns. It wasn't an alien. Just a cow.

GOLDEN RETRIEVER

Leo stayed at school that day and it was the same as always. He sat off the mat in class and hid under the stairs at lunch. When Dad picked him up, a few kids waved to Peg, who was sitting in the back seat. Dad must have seen it because he started filling the car with questions. They weren't big questions like Leo's, just ordinary ones.

'So, buddy. Have a good day? Anything exciting happen? Learn anything new? Anyone say anything funny?'

Leo yawned. He only wanted to answer

one of the questions. 'We read a book about chameleons.' His words crawled out. 'They turn dark when they're cold and pale when they're sick.'

'Yeah, wow.' Dad nodded a lot. 'Wow.'

But Leo didn't want to think about chameleons. They reminded him of the coloured animals on the chart. He wanted to think about something else, so he looked out the window, up at the sky. It was the colour of dirty concrete. He could smell rain.

'Cute!' Peg pointed out the window at a dog sniffing around a letterbox. 'What sort is it?'

'Golden retriever.' Dad knew a lot about dogs from his drawings. 'Pretty young too.'

Leo stared at the dog as it snuffled its nose in the grass. Its fur really was golden, like the sun when it first peeped over the trees. He imagined running his fingers along its back and scruffing the hair around its ears. Before he'd lost himself in space, he had lots of wonders about dogs. How did they know the time of day? How many human words did they know?

They left the retriever behind and rolled through the suburb under the grey sky. Clouds bubbled and brewed. As Dad parked in the driveway, the sky cracked open and rain rushed down. Heavy drops hit Leo's head as he ran to the house. Mum arrived soon after. She shook off her jacket and towelled her hair dry. Then she and Dad stirred cups of hot cocoa for everyone. Leo watched the steam swirl out of his cup but, before he realised what was happening, his parents were talking about the coloured animals again. Which animal had he felt like today? Did he see other kids being red bulls or white mice? What could they do to help him feel like a happy yellow songbird?

A hundred questions later, Mum sighed. She held his hand. It was warm from the cup. 'Sorry, love. You probably just want to be left alone. It's just ... you have all those big thoughts in your head. If you keep them to yourself, the world misses out and you do too. Don't you think it'd be great to share it all with a friend?'

Leo slurped his cocoa. 'Yeah. I guess.' He wasn't sure if it was true or if he wanted the talking to stop.

Dad joined in. 'Good on you, bud. We can help. And Mrs Lloyd is there too. Just keep at it. You'll find someone in your own way.'

Leo nodded. He was tired of this. He had to find a way to make Mum's wish come true. If he just had someone to play with, everything would be okay and he wouldn't have to worry about Mrs Lloyd's coloured animals, or everyone liking Peg, or Mum and Dad whispering about him in the lounge room at night. But how would it happen? Talking to other kids didn't work, and neither did joining in their games. If he was going to make a friend, there had to be another way.

THE BALLOON RETURNS

When Leo woke the next morning, the rain had stopped. He opened his curtains and it was beautiful outside. The grass glistened. A bird sang on the fence. The sky had shaken off its grey coat and was bright blue again. Something caught his eye through the branches of their backyard tree. It was small, round and white, and moving too fast to be the daytime moon.

'The white balloon,' he whispered.

As soon as he spoke, it disappeared. Lost behind the canopy of the tree. He waited and watched and it soon came back, glimpsed through a loose patchwork of leaves. Something hung from its ribbon, a strange shape, some sort of animal.

It vanished again.

He waited and waited but it didn't come back. It must have blown to the other side of the city, the other side of the world. He sat on his bed and tried to forget about it. It was Saturday, so he didn't have to get ready for school. He could sit in his room all day and make more aliens for the album. Maybe he could watch another show about—

THUMP!

Something hit the house, right outside his room. He ran to the window, stuck his head out and looked down. There was nothing on the ground. Then he lifted his head. The white balloon was stuck in the tree, caught neatly in a forked branch. Its shiny ribbon dangled in the breeze.

He sprinted outside in his pyjama shorts, ran over to the tree and started to climb.

The branches were wet from the rain. His feet slipped and he scratched his knee. A line of blood trickled down his leg, but he kept going, heaving himself up through the branches until he reached the balloon. He stretched out, tapped it free and snatched at the ribbon. But it slipped through his fingers and the balloon bobbed away, clear of the tree and the roof of the house. It sailed higher, found an unseen current in the air and, in a flash, it flew away.

He crept back down the tree, careful not to slip, and went inside. No one else was awake. They must have slept through the whole thing, even the thump on the house. He wandered down the hallway, thought about falling back into bed, but stopped outside his door.

There was a noise. Shuffling. And breathing. Like an animal sniffing around the room.

His heart pounded as he creaked open the door.

Nothing. Then he edged the door further, took a step into the room and saw it.

A strange shaggy creature, a bit shorter than he was, stood by the window. It had long flappy ears, two stubby horns, and arms and legs like soft pointy socks. On its face was a pair of sparkly eyes and a big round nose like a bulgy mushroom. Leo grinned. He had never seen this thing before, but he knew what it was.

Mum's wish had come true.

A FRIEND

Leo moved closer to the creature. He swallowed. Stretched out his hand and touched the honey-coloured fur. It was soft, like the hair of a golden retriever. The creature didn't move at first. It was like an oversized toy. Then an ear twitched, both horns wiggled and it tilted its head.

Leo coughed. 'Hello?'

It smiled with sparkly eyes and flapped its ears.

'You came down with the balloon.' Leo knew it was true, but he still waited until the creature nodded. 'And you hit the house. Are you okay?'

It nodded again and twitched its horns.

'But how—' Leo leant out the window, as he had done earlier that morning. It was a long way down to the ground. 'How did you get in here? You must be a good climber.'

The creature looked around the room. It darted to the wardrobe and scampered up the shelves like a furry monkey until it sat on top, much higher than Leo could reach, or climb.

'Wow.' Leo bounced on his toes. 'What else can you do?'

His shaggy friend slid down the wardrobe, took a breath, then rolled a somersault across the carpet. It wasn't as impressive as the climbing, but Leo still clapped like he'd seen a magic trick. Then the creature raised its hairy sock arms, paused, and folded forwards into a handstand. But it teetered, overbalanced and tumbled to the floor. Leo helped it up and noticed something different. Its flappy ears hung down, the stubby horns drooped, but strangest of all, its fur changed colour, from yellowy-gold to stone grey.

'Don't worry. I can't do handstands either. Watch.' Leo rocked forward into his own handstand but tipped over and crashed to the carpet. 'See? Maybe we're both too short.'

The creature's face melted into a smile and a warm yellow returned to its fur. The colours seemed to match its mood, like the animals on Mrs Lloyd's chart.

'Wanna see my album?' Leo grabbed the book and they sat together on the bed. His friend swung his little sock feet as Leo pointed to the front cover. 'That says *Friends*.' Then he turned the pages and showed him the different aliens. 'This is a Gronk. That's a Zot. And this one here – this is an Umph.' He closed the book and faced the creature. 'You're an alien too, right?'

It flapped its ears and smiled.

'I know – I'll take your photo!'

Leo found the camera and positioned his friend in the frame. He pressed the shutter and the photograph zipped out. But his furry friend wasn't in the picture – only the messy bed where it was supposed to be. He shook his head, but he understood. This alien wasn't a ghost. It wasn't invisible. It was just something that no one else could see, not even a camera. Only Leo could picture it on his bed, or climbing the wardrobe, or dangling from a balloon in the sky. But the thought didn't sink Leo – it lifted him, like he was a balloon full of air himself. This was a friend just for him.

He was twitchy and excited. He wriggled his toes and waggled his fingers and tried to think of something friends would do. 'Want to play a game?'

The alien sprang off the bed and danced from foot to foot.

'Why don't we play—' Leo stopped. His friend hadn't said a word. 'Can you talk?'

The alien widened its eyes and wiggled its big round nose. Then it opened its mouth and a warm growly voice came out. 'Yes,' it said. 'I can talk.'

‘Oh,’ said Leo. ‘You just hadn’t said anything yet.’

His friend gave a small shrug. ‘I didn’t want to butt in.’

Before he realised what he was doing, Leo hugged the alien. It was the best hug and he didn’t want to let go.

Finally, his friend stepped back. ‘I know a game that you’ll like. And it doesn’t have any volcanoes.’

Leo laughed. The air nearly burst out of his chest. Then the two friends bundled out of the room, down the stairs and into the yard to play.

RALPH

The game was called Asteroids. It was simple, but Leo loved it. They collected ten coloured rocks from the garden and then took turns hiding them around the yard. One player had to find them before the other counted to fifty. The alien was especially good at Asteroids. His pointy sock hands could reach into small hiding places, and he was much better than Leo at climbing trees.

They played over and over. Leo's head was sweaty, his feet were grubby, but he kept playing. For once, he knew the rules of a game and his short legs did what they were supposed to. As he puffed around the yard, hunting for the rocks, someone called out from the house.

'Leo!' It was Mum, standing on the top step. 'What are you doing?'

He stopped running and squinted up at her. The sun was in his eyes. 'Playing.'

'In your pyjamas?'

He looked down at his pyjama shorts. The dried blood on his leg reminded him of all that had happened that morning. Then he felt something brush against him. The little alien was beside him. Leo stuck out his pinky finger and his friend held on.

Mum walked down the steps. Her dressing gown was wrapped tight and she held a cup of coffee. 'What's going on? What are you playing?'

He scratched the back of his head. 'A game. It's called Asteroids.'

'Oh.' She blew steam from the cup. 'How do you play?'

'You, well, you hide these.' He pointed to his pile of coloured rocks. 'And then someone has to find them.'

She sipped her coffee. 'That sounds like a game for more than one person.'

It wasn't a question, but Leo knew he had to say something. 'I was playing with …' He felt a squeeze on his finger. 'I was playing with my friend.'

She wrapped her hands around the cup and looked at him without blinking. Then her gaze travelled down and landed on his pinky finger stuck out to the side. 'What are you doing?'

'It's my friend. It's holding on to my finger.'

A small crease appeared between her eyes. She looked from the finger to Leo's face, then to the space beside him. The friend bounced on its hairy sock feet and wriggled its bumpy horns. But all Mum would have seen was the empty space.

'You've made a friend,' she said slowly. 'An imaginary friend.'

The sun hit his face harder, and everything was itchy. He still felt like a blown-up balloon but one that was ready to pop. He shouldn't have told her. Should have kept it to himself. But then the sun softened behind a cloud and the line between Mum's eyes disappeared.

She took another sip and she smiled. 'I want to know all about it.'

So he talked about the mushroom nose and the flappy ears and the cute little horns on top. He told her about the hands and feet like hairy socks and the way the fur changed colour. The words spilled out like never before and he kept going, describing the warm growly voice and the way it climbed.

Mum's eyes were wet, and her face was shiny and red. 'It sounds perfect, love. Does it feel good to have someone?'

'Yeah. You were right.'

She held his hand. 'Have you thought of a name?'

'No, not yet. But I think it's a boy.'

His friend leant into him and nodded.

There was a sweet, faraway look in her eyes. 'How about *Ralph*?'

Leo whispered the name. 'Ralph.' It made his mouth move round like a circle, and he liked the soft furry sound at the end. It was just right.

RALPHORA

Ralph became the best friend Leo could have ever imagined. They did everything together and Leo even took him to school. They sat side by side on the colourful mat. Built UFOs at the construction table. They played Asteroids next to the oval, hiding and finding their coloured rocks. They stayed clear of the other kids because Leo didn't need to try anymore. He had a friend who made him laugh, who didn't butt in and who gave the best hugs.

At lunchtimes, the two friends huddled in the spot under the office stairs, sharing sandwiches and secrets. Leo loved hearing Ralph's stories about space.

'You should see Jupiter,' said Ralph. 'It's huge!'

'Wow.' Leo chomped into his cheese sandwich. 'You've really seen it up close?'

'Yeah. That's where I'm from.'

'You're from Jupiter?'

Ralph shook his head. 'One of its moons. It's called Ralphora.'

Leo smiled with a mouthful of bread and cheese. 'Ralph from Ralphora. What's it like there?'

'Amazing! The trees are made of fairy floss and the rivers are full of pink lemonade.'

Leo closed his eyes and rolled back. 'Yum!' He licked his lips and rubbed his belly.

Ralph talked more about his home. All the aliens there were like him but different shapes and sizes – some short and round, others tall and a bit wonky. When they were old enough, the Ralphs travelled to other planets so they could help other creatures, including humans. That was why Ralph was here. He had zipped through space, all the way to Earth, to be with Leo because he didn't have a friend.

'Do you miss Ralphora?'

'A bit,' said Ralph. 'But I like it here.'

Leo took the last bite of his sandwich. 'And will you stay forever?'

It was a big question. Ralph gazed skyward and his golden fur faded. 'As long as you need me.'

Leo smiled. He would always need Ralph.

GAMES

Mum liked Ralph from the start. She asked about him and smiled whenever she spotted Leo's pinky finger stuck out to the side. The rest of the family took a bit longer. Peg said it made no sense. Dad scratched his head and twisted his mouth whenever Leo mentioned him. But after some prodding from Mum, they all agreed to make room for Ralph in their lives. Dad set a fifth place at the table. Peg left the beanbag free. And they all waited for an extra seatbelt click before Mum or Dad backed out of the driveway.

Mrs Lloyd didn't seem to notice Ralph straightaway. In the noisy world of a Prep room, it was easy to hide an imaginary friend. But after a few weeks, Mum and Dad told her about the addition to her class. He wasn't the first imaginary friend she'd taught, so Ralph was welcome to stay. 'If that's what makes Leo happy,' she said, 'then that's what we'll do.'

With Ralph by his side, the weeks and months rocketed by. They stuck together at home and at school, inventing more games to play. A simple one was Bounce the Moon, in which they kept a balloon up for as long as possible, without letting it touch the ground. They could use any part of their body to keep it afloat, and Leo loved it whenever the balloon got stuck between Ralph's stumpy horns.

Another game was Moon Walk. They turned old paint tins into moon boots and stomped through an outer space obstacle course in the backyard. They used an old wheelbarrow as space junk, shovelled holes for craters, and threw fluffy toys to make a meteor shower. That was Ralph's favourite part. He would stand with his paws stretched out, getting pummelled by teddies, like he was soaking up a summer rainstorm.

At bedtime, with all the lights off, Leo and Ralph cuddled in bed and looked out the window. Sometimes Ralph talked about Ralphora. Other nights, Leo would imagine lines between the stars to make up his own constellations. Most of the time, they didn't talk. Just lay together and gazed at the never-ending darkness. Occasionally, if they were lucky, a shooting star would whip through the sky. Whenever that happened, Leo closed his eyes and wished to be this happy forever.

THE TELESCOPE

Later in the year, Leo stopped at the post office window. There was a telescope on display, pointed at a corner of the ceiling.

'We can't get it today,' Mum said. 'But if we save a little each week …'

His nose was pressed against the glass. 'What if Dad mows more lawns?'

'I don't think—'

'Could *you* mow some lawns?'

She laughed. 'I could, but I'm a bit busy being a teacher.'

He counted the weeks as they passed –

seven, eight, nine – and then one afternoon, he came home to the telescope set up in his room. He hugged Mum and Dad and took a closer look. It was as long as a teacher's ruler, came with a tripod and fitted into a carry bag he could sling over his shoulder. The first night he had it, he took it outside to the yard. He spread a blanket on the grass and pulled the corners tight. Then he fixed the telescope to the tripod, sat down with Ralph, and looked through the eyepiece. The sky was painted deep blue and, through the lens, the stars appeared, like tiny eyes opening up.

The back door squeaked. Leo turned and saw Mum, Dad and Peg standing in the doorway, like someone had squashed them all into a skinny photo frame.

'What can you see?' said Mum.

'Stars.'

'Anything else?' said Peg.

'Not yet.'

Mum and Peg went back inside.

Dad waited. He was still in his mowing clothes. 'You there with Ralph?'

'Yeah,' said Leo. Ralph was holding his finger.

Dad went inside, but a moment later he walked down the steps, carrying a sleeping bag and two pillows. He dropped them on the blanket. 'Don't want to get cold, buddy.'

'Thanks.' Leo stuffed a pillow under his head. 'Did the telescope cost a lot?'

Dad stood with his hands in his pockets. He jiggled his leg, but he didn't say anything.

'Will we have to live in a tent?'

Dad laughed. 'Don't worry, bud.' He went back inside.

Finally, it was just Leo and Ralph. A cat miaowed from a nearby yard and the air grew cool. They sat with the sleeping bag wrapped around their shoulders and took turns to peer through the telescope at the glittery sky. They swung the scope from star to star and then spotted Venus hanging low above the trees.

The best thing to track was the moon. Through the lens, they saw the splotchy surface, covered in craters. Leo could almost touch it.

'Is that what Ralphora looks like?'

Ralph closed one eye and peeked through the lens. 'It's just as nice. But Ralphora is more colourful.' His fur turned a mischievous orange and he panned the telescope in a different direction. 'See that star there, straight up from the streetlight?' His voice was husky and bright. 'Imagine it was a planet where the aliens looked like giant doughnuts, all with different coloured icing. They wouldn't walk – they'd bounce. And they'd all want to eat each other.'

Leo's face brightened like the moon. This was why he was friends with Ralph. They made up more funny planets, pointing them out with the telescope – a milkshake planet, a tiny elephant planet, and another with aliens like kernels of corn that popped into popcorn if they got mad. They thought of alien names too. Bollybops. Dinkles. Ooks. Leo's favourites were the Grimbles, the backwards-talking aliens from the planet Flumblebot.

The two friends practised talking the same way.

'Name your is what?'

'Leo is … name my.'

They giggled and tried another one.

'Friend your is who?'

'Ralph is … friend … best my.'

They fell on the blanket and laughed.

The next night, they took the telescope to the backyard and did the same thing. They called the game Other Worlds and they played it almost every night. All they needed was a clear sky, the telescope and an armful of blankets and pillows. When they went to bed, the last thing they said was the Grimble way of saying goodnight.

'Tomorrow you see.'

'Tomorrow you see.'

Leo would drift to sleep with Ralph on one side and the telescope on the other.

ALIEN SHIPS

Life with Ralph rolled along. Prep came to an end and Year 1 arrived with a short, serious teacher called Ms Umber. When she first heard about Ralph, she folded her arms tight and glared at Leo with cardboard-brown eyes.

'Ralph. Spelt R-A-L-P-H?'

Leo gulped. 'Yes.'

'Good. Make him a name tag. Stick it on his desk. But if I hear one peep from your furry little friend, if he interrupts me just once, he'll be out, lickety-split.' She winked. 'Understand?'

Leo had never heard 'lickety-split' before, but he nodded yes.

Year 2 wheeled by with Mr Pole, a thin, tired man who wrote the wrong date on the board almost every day. Then Leo was in Year 3, a head taller than when he had started Prep but still smaller than everyone else. His teacher was a gentle woman called Mrs Lavender. She spoke just above a whisper and her classroom was the quietest he had ever known. He and Ralph loved it. She had even had her own imaginary friend as a child.

'She wasn't an alien,' Mrs Lavender said. 'She was a girl like me but much louder and wilder. Her name was Beatrix.'

In the few years that had passed, two things had deepened for Leo: his friendship with Ralph and his interest in space. They still played some of their games, but as Leo's reading improved, they explored the universe more through books. Leo knew all the constellations, could recite details of almost every space mission, and had researched alien encounters around the world. He loved reading about UFO sightings the most. He remembered the white balloon from the day Ralph arrived, but he longed to see a real alien ship. It would answer his biggest wonderings and outshine all the imagining he had done in his life.

'The ships on Ralphora look like giant soccer balls,' said Ralph.

'Can they fly anywhere?'

'Almost. They don't come all the way to the ground. If you want to catch a Ralphora ship, you have to climb up high first.'

'How high?' Leo looked around for tall things. 'The roof of the house?'

Ralph gave a thoughtful frown. 'Much higher. You'd have to climb to the top of a building, then a ship could pick you up.'

Leo thought of the buildings he had seen in the city, so tall they made him dizzy. What would it be like to stand on top as an enormous soccer ball rolled down from above? 'I'd love to see one.'

‘A ship from Ralphora?’

‘Yeah.’

Ralph’s horns drooped. ‘No you wouldn’t.’

‘Why?’

‘Because if you ever see a Ralphora ship—’ He paused, then shook his head. ‘Never mind.’

He talked about ships from other parts of space. Some looked like Frisbees, others like pumpkins, and one looked like a pencil, with a pointy tip and a rubber on the end.

Leo spent more and more time with the telescope. Daytime or nighttime, at school and at home, he stared through the eyepiece at blank patches of sky, hoping a strange shape would fly into view. Ralph stuck by his side, but the other students kept well away. Leo didn’t mind. He liked looking up and the kids were just blurry shapes on the ground. Now and then, Mum and Dad tried to steer him towards other children, dragging him to a birthday party or inviting people over. Peg sometimes lured him to a board game or a TV show. He would be polite, but he never lasted long. So everyone left him to the things that made him happy: Ralph, the telescope and the endless world above.

THE PICTURE FRAME

One Saturday morning, Leo and Peg were in the kitchen. Leo was stirring a cup of chocolate milk while Peg smeared jam onto a piece of bread. Mum and Dad were talking in the next room.

'We have to do something,' Mum said. 'Can you do any more yards?'

'Maybe.' Dad was quiet, like he didn't want his voice to go very far. 'I could do more on the weekends. But I can't make the grass grow any faster.'

Leo added more chocolate powder and Peg folded her bread in half.

Mum sighed. 'There's not much more *I* can do. The only way I could get a promotion is to move to a smaller school, away from the city.'

Peg was about to bite into her sandwich. 'What's a promotion?'

Leo kept his voice quieter than Dad's. 'Bigger job, I think. More money.'

She took a bite and chewed slowly.

Dad's whispery voice wandered from the other room. 'Do you think we could move? I mean, the kids—'

'Peg would be okay, but …'

Peg held her sandwich still and Leo stopped stirring. The rest of Mum's sentence never came. Maybe she had realised they were listening. Or she might have given Dad one of her looks, so they didn't need to use words. Leo gulped his drink down, dropped the cup in the sink and ran to his room to find Ralph.

He was sitting on top of the cupboard, swinging his legs.

Leo pulled a packet of balloons from his desk. 'Bounce the Moon?'

Ralph jumped down and landed on the carpet with a clumsy roll. Leo blew up a balloon and they started tapping it around the room. They leapt off the bed, climbed on the desk chair and Ralph swung from the ceiling fan. Leo hit the balloon harder and harder, trying to swat Mum and Dad's conversation out of his head.

They took the game into the hallway and then the lounge room, smacking the balloon all the way. Hurtled across the couch, dived into the beanbag and tumbled along the floor to keep the moon from touching the ground. Then Leo hurled himself off an armchair, lunged at the balloon and knocked a framed picture off its hook. It skidded down the wall and hit the floor with a crack.

Mum rushed in. 'Are you okay?'

He was lying on the carpet. His chest heaved up and down. 'Yeah. But the picture …'

She picked it up and sat in the armchair. He got to his feet and squeezed in next to her. It was a drawing of a black-and-white dog. A corner of the frame had come apart and the glass was cracked into three pieces.

'Sorry. Ralph and I were playing.' He was still puffed. 'That's one of Dad's pictures.'

She put her arm around him. 'As long as you're not hurt.'

'Only this.' He showed her a patch of carpet burn on his elbow. 'He's gonna be mad, isn't he.'

'He might be worried. Ralph's a good friend, love. He's made you so happy. But we don't want you getting hurt or getting yourself into trouble.'

Leo pushed himself out of the armchair. Now Mum had thrown another worry into the air. He picked up the balloon and slouched back to his room. Ralph followed, dishwater-grey. They lay on the bed with the telescope between them and waited for night to come.

THE FARM

For the next few weeks, Leo fell deeper into his alien daydreams, chatting to Ralph and searching the skies. He found a small mound of dirt near the back of the school, away from tall trees, and set up his telescope there most lunchtimes. One day, he was looking at an empty piece of the sky when someone tapped his shoulder.

'Hey.'

He turned. A girl stood with her hands on her hips. She had short dark hair and her cheeks were red as if she'd been running.

'What?'

'Mrs Lavender told me to get you.'

He blinked. He couldn't remember this girl. 'Why?'

She rolled her eyes. 'Because you're late. Lunchtime is over.'

He hadn't heard the bell. Didn't notice the oval and playground had emptied. He packed the telescope and tripod into its sleeve and followed the girl back to class.

It happened a few times each week after that. He lost himself in the sky and missed the bell. Every time, a kid would tap him on the shoulder and lead him back to Mrs Lavender. Mum and Dad found out and he promised to stay closer to the classroom and listen for the bell. Then something terrible happened near the end of Year 3.

The students were learning about life cycles and Mrs Lavender took them to a farm outside the city. As they stepped off the bus, the sun lit up the fields and the stench of manure filled the air. The class wandered from paddock to pen, and the teacher talked about the stages of life, but her voice was lost in the babble of children gushing at the baby animals. Grubby piglets that grunted, fluffy chicks that skittered and squeaked, and clumsy foals with knobbly knees that tried to keep up with their mothers.

Leo and Ralph fell behind the group. From the moment they arrived, Leo was lost in the sky. It appeared so big, away from the buildings and trees and power poles of the city. All these years he had been looking up, he had never seen this much of that empty blue above the world. He found an open square of dirt, unzipped his telescope and aimed it at the sky. Wished more than anything to spot a UFO.

When nothing appeared, he packed the telescope away and looked for his class. But there was no one around. He had lost track of them, had missed one of Mrs Lavender's quiet instructions. He couldn't even hear kids' voices.

Now he was stranded in a square pen, bordered by a rough wooden fence. No idea how he got there and no idea where to go. A bird squawked from the roof of a shed. Flies buzzed at some brown sludge near his foot. Then a deep rumbly snort shook the ground and Leo's body quivered and quaked.

He turned around. Ralph grabbed his finger.

Inside the pen was a pig. Enormous and hairy, as tall as Ralph and as wide as a wheelbarrow. It was so huge it looked like it had been made by mushing all the other pigs together. It grunted again, stomped the dirt and tracked Leo with its wet black eyes. A thick line of drool swung from its snout.

'On the count of three,' Leo whispered, 'we run.'

Ralph nodded and his ears twitched. His fur was murky purple.

'One.'

The pig stepped closer.

'Two.'

It took another step and snorted a spray of snot.

'Three.'

Leo and Ralph turned and bolted for the fence. The pig let out an ear-splitting squeal and barrelled after them, like a cement truck on legs, kicking up a cloud of dust. Leo's shoes thumped on the dirt as he sprinted. Ralph spurted ahead, like a big furry basketball hurtling across the pen. The pig was closer now, ploughing towards Leo, and the earth shuddered under its trotters. They were nearly at the fence. Ralph got there first, sprang up and tumbled over.

Leo strained to reach it. The pig was right behind him. A metre from the fence, Leo jumped, clung to a splintered post and scrambled to the top. But the pig didn't stop. It smashed into the wooden rails and Leo was bucked off. He flipped through the air like a stuffed toy flung from a bridge and landed – *WHACK!* – on the ground. Something snuffled nearby – the pig? Ralph crying? – and the world was a slow-moving blur. A smudged purple shape came into view, and he guessed it was Ralph. The last thing he remembered was a sharp throbbing pain that flooded his right side, then he closed his eyes and couldn't feel anything at all.

CHANGES

Hospital wasn't much fun. Leo had his own room with a TV suspended from the ceiling, but there was too much noise. Trolleys rattled down hallways. Machines beeped from other rooms. Patients coughed and nurses talked. Mum was snoring softly in a small bed next to him, but he was never going to get to sleep. Of course, Mum didn't have a twisted knee, a body full of bruises and an arm in plaster like he did. At least Ralph was there with him, sharing his pillow in the strange hospital bed.

He was still awake when a bowl of cereal was plonked in front of him. A nurse arrived with a loud voice, scribbled notes on a clipboard, then Leo and Mum were allowed to go home. He slept in the car, sleepwalked into the house and collapsed onto the bed.

A few days later, he sat in his room, turning the telescope in his hands. It was injured from the farm too: a dent in the side, rattly eyepiece and a thin crack on the lens. When Mum and Dad came in, he wanted to ask if someone could fix it, but they sat either side of him with tight looks on their faces. Ralph flushed a nervous green.

'Can we talk,' said Mum, 'about what happened?'

Dad scratched the back of his head. 'It was Ralph, wasn't it.' His words shot out faster than Mum's. 'That's why you got stuck in that pen. He led you astray.'

Leo felt hot. His eyes stung. 'It wasn't Ralph's fault. I was looking for—'

'Leo, love. You're not in trouble.' Mum looked at Dad, as if to remind him too. 'We know how special Ralph is. We're just worried that he might be causing some problems.'

'Nothing like this has happened before,' he said.

'Not quite.' Mum rubbed her palms together. The crease appeared between her eyes. 'There was the picture frame. And you've been forgetting to go back to class. Whenever someone finds you, you're in your own world, talking to Ralph.'

'And he's stopped you from making friends,' said Dad.

Leo sat up and kicked off the blankets. 'He *is* my friend!'

'Imaginary,' said Dad.

'Still my friend.'

'We know,' said Mum. 'But you're getting older. You've nearly finished Year 3. And there'll be a few changes next year and, well, we've been thinking ...'

Leo wriggled his fingers sticking out the bottom of the plaster cast. 'What changes?'

Dad took over. He said something about money. He couldn't fit in any more lawns, Mum had been trying for bigger jobs in the city, but now they didn't have much choice.

Leo picked at the plaster. 'What about your pictures? Can't you sell some?'

'No one wants those, bud.'

Leo wondered what was coming. He'd have to sell his telescope. They'd have to live in a tent.

Then Mum locked her hands together and told him her news. She had taken a new job as a deputy principal. It was a small high school in a small town, a place called Dundle.

'Never heard of Dundle,' said Leo.

'None of us have,' laughed Dad.

'But it looks sweet – a little country town.' Mum held Leo's unplastered hand. 'You and Peg will be at the primary school, and I'll be at the high school. It'll mean more money and it's a cheaper place to live, so Dad can take a break from mowing yards. It's pretty dry out there, so there won't be much grass anyway.'

Leo nodded, but a small weight of worry, the size of a pumpkin seed, sprouted in his chest. It grew like a vine and snaked inside him as Mum spoke again.

'You'll be in Year 4. New school, new kids.' She smiled with wet eyes. 'It might be time to say goodbye to Ralph.'

The worry vine exploded into a tangled knot of tendrils and thorns, prickling his insides. This was the real reason they wanted to move – not money or jobs or country towns. They wanted him to leave Ralph behind and start all over again, just because he'd been chased by a pig.

'I can't.' It came out like an angry whisper. 'I can't say goodbye.'

'I know you don't want to, but we'll help,' Mum said. 'We'll make a plan so it all works out. I promise.'

He wiped a tear with his sleeve. Mum and Dad hugged him and said a few more things, but he wasn't really listening. Peg came in to show him where Dundle lay on a map, but he didn't pay attention to that, either. He just sat in bed, nursing his cast, with Mum's words echoing in his head. For so long she had wished for him to find a friend. Now he had to say goodbye.

THE PROMISE

Leo had to make a plan. Some things couldn't be stopped: they were definitely moving and he had to say goodbye to Ralph. But if the two friends thought hard enough, they'd find a way to lessen the hurt. The whole thing scared him and his fear came out in silly ideas.

'I could squash you into my suitcase,' he said. 'Or you could hide in the boot under all the bags.'

It was the last week of Year 3. Leo sat in his spot under the office stairs, chewing a crumbly biscuit. Ralph lay on one of the steps with his head poking through a gap, so the two of them could still see each other.

'Squash me into a suitcase? Hide me in the boot? That's how you treat your best friend?' He closed his eyes and sniffed.

Leo giggled. 'I've got it! You could catch a balloon or a spaceship – your big soccer ball spaceship – and follow us to Dundle. Then you could disguise yourself as a new kid at school, like me.' He cracked up at the thought of Ralph in a collared shirt and bucket hat. Crumbs flew out of his mouth.

Ralph slid through the gap in the steps, flipped upside down and landed, right way up, next to him. 'This isn't a joke.'

Leo wiped his mouth with the back of his hand. 'Yeah, sorry.'

It happened like this sometimes. One of them was serious while the other messed around.

'And you really don't get how those spaceships work.'

Leo fished for something else in his lunchbox. 'What do you mean?'

Ralph took a deep breath. 'I can't just grab a balloon and fly away. I can't call the UFO pilots and ask them to pick me up. I'm not in charge of any of those things.'

Leo left his lunchbox alone.

Ralph's fur turned deep blue, like the bottom of the ocean. 'Remember when I said I hope you never see a ship from Ralphora?'

'Yeah.'

'It's because ... if one of my ships comes to get me, you'll never see me again. It'll be goodbye forever, and not because your parents said so. I'll be gone because you won't need me anymore.'

Leo scuffed the concrete with his shoe. 'That won't ever happen. I'll always need you.'

Ralph didn't say anything. He looked down and swung his legs. The school bell rang and the buzz of the playground died away as everyone ran into classrooms. Leo had to join them.

He didn't want the school to call his parents again. But he had to work this out.

He climbed out of his hiding spot. 'What will happen to you when I go to Dundle?'

'Doesn't matter,' said Ralph. 'Your parents told you to say goodbye, so that's what we'll do.'

'But you won't disappear in a big soccer ball just yet?'

He shook his furry head.

'Good,' said Leo. 'I've got an idea.'

He told Ralph the plan. Ralph wasn't sure at first, but Leo talked him around. They made their secret promise, gathered Leo's lunch things, then raced back to the classroom before they got into trouble.

☆

The big goodbye happened about a month later. They played Other Worlds for the last time. Pointed the cracked telescope at the spaces between stars and laughed about the Grimbles from Flumblebot. Then they hugged, said their backwards goodbyes and Leo dropped the telescope in the bin. He had never felt so sad. But deep in his heart, he carried the promise he had made with Ralph. It glowed softly in the dark, like a distant star.

THE DRIVE

Leo stared out the car window as they drove to their new home. Mum and Dad said it would take ten hours, maybe eleven. He hadn't seen even a photo of the house. He only knew that Dundle was a small town, a tiny black dot on the orangey-brown part of Peg's map. They'd always lived in the green corner of the map, close to the city, not far from the beach. Now they sped along a bumpy highway towards the orangey-brown, away from everything he knew and away from Ralph.

Peg sat across from him on the back seat. She caught him looking at her. 'What?'

'Nothing,' he said. 'Whatcha thinking about?'

She stared out the window. 'Clouds. See that big fluffy one?' She pointed to the sky. 'What do you think it looks like?'

He stretched across the seat and looked out her window. Any other day he would have said it was something from space. A Gronk or a Grimble. A marshmallow planet. But not today. 'It looks like a turtle.'

She angled her head. 'I thought it was a cow. Anyway, there won't be many clouds in Dundle. Dad said it never rains.'

There was nothing else on the highway, then a dot appeared in the distance, straight ahead. It grew bigger as it came towards them on the other side of the road and Leo saw it was a huge truck. When it roared past them, as loud as a hailstorm, it felt like their car might blow off the road.

Peg turned to Leo. 'I can't stop thinking about school, either – who my teacher will be, what the kids'll be like.'

'Yeah.' Leo winced at the thought of school. His chance to start again, like Mum and Dad said. Leave Ralph behind and find someone real.

She tapped his head. 'What are *you* thinking about?'

He wrinkled his nose. 'Not much.'

'I thought you'd be thinking about Ralph.'

'Well.' He faced his own window. 'Yeah. A bit.'

He had thought about nothing else for the whole drive. With every small town they passed, a memory of Ralph flashed in his mind. They drove past a rusty ute in Wilcott and he thought of the day he and Ralph carved a dirt track for his toy cars. A girl cycled along a path in Craven Creek and he remembered riding his bike along a forest trail, Ralph clinging to his back the whole time. The towns whizzed by and he daydreamed of all they had done together. Climbing trees, making cubbies and swimming like a pair of sea otters.

After dinner in Mount Logan, Dad said there was only an hour left till they got there. Leo let his head fall against the car window. The sinking sun spilled apricot and plum into the sky. Silhouettes of sleeping cows rested in paddocks and, out Peg's window, a field of sunflowers caught the last breath of light. The car tyres hummed and the song on the radio dissolved into fuzz. Leo closed his eyes and yawned. The last thing he heard was Peg snuffle and snore, and it reminded him of Ralph's sniffly nose when they'd said goodbye.

HOME

Leo woke as sunlight flooded through a window beside his bed. He squinted at the white walls, the corner closet and the pedestal fan that creaked with every half-turn. A huge pine tree stood outside the window and, beyond that, a line of high wooden houses baked in the sun. There was so much space between them compared to the houses back home.

Home. The word tugged at his insides. It meant something else now. Home was this wide window, that giant pine, these bright, white walls. He rolled out of bed, rubbed his eyes and wandered from room to room. It was an old house made of tall timber walls with big windows on hinges, and it smelt of fresh paint. There was greeny-blue carpet, lino in the kitchen and a verandah that stretched from one end of the house to the other. That was where he found Mum and Dad, sipping coffee at a wooden table.

'Hey, sleepyhead.' The sunlight hit Dad's face. 'What do you think?'

Dad nodded towards the view. There was a patchy soccer field, a bunch of two-storey buildings with louvre windows, and a tall sign that said something about the start of the school term.

'Wait a minute.' Leo wiped the sleep from his eyes. 'Are we … living in the school?'

'Bingo,' said Dad. 'The high school.'

'In towns like this, teachers sometimes live in a house on the school grounds,' said Mum. 'So that's me. That's us. Here we are.'

Leo had been in empty schools before,

waiting for Mum to finish meetings. It always felt odd, like a night sky without stars.

She must have read his face. 'I know it's hard, love. But you'll get used to it. Everything feels strange when it's new.'

Silence hung between them.

Dad rested his cup on the table and rubbed his hands together. 'Come on, then. Let's get dressed and hit the town.'

THE TOWN

The map was right. Dundle was orange-brown. And oven-hot. As Leo stood with his family on the footpath of the main street, he felt like a blob of dough crisping into a biscuit. Or a square of chocolate melting into sticky goo. Either way, he was going to burn or evaporate if he stayed on the footpath for much longer.

'It's so hot.' Peg's face flushed.

'Thirty-six degrees,' said Mum. She tucked a sweaty strand of hair behind her ear.

'Well, we're here.' Dad swatted a fly from

his nose. 'We may as well look around. Then we'll find the town pool.'

Leo followed his family down the street. The shops were plain and square, with sliding doors covered in faded posters, and wide roofs that shaded the footpath. There was a bakery, lots of hair salons and a cafe with white plastic chairs. The grocery shop wasn't as shiny as the ones Leo had known and the saddlery was like nothing he had ever seen, full of stirrups, straps and the thick smell of leather.

They reached the last block of shops and walked past houses surrounded by dead grass and dirt. All the yards were the same, flat brown squares that multiplied to make the town, like a big dusty chessboard. There was no one in the yards. No pets, either. Everyone was probably hiding inside, afraid to step into the blazing heat.

At the end of the street was an empty lagoon, nothing more than a wide ditch of weeds. A path ran around the outside and a strange tower stood on the other side. It was as tall as some of the gum trees.

'What's that?' Leo said.

No one heard him. The family were already walking back, so he took another look at the tower, then turned and caught up.

They walked back along the main street under the blistering sun. By the time they made it to the car, Leo's hat was drenched in sweat and he'd given up shooing the flies that covered his shirt. He collapsed on the back seat and let the air-con blast cold wind in his face.

They drove slowly and the blocks of houses rolled past like old photos: dull and brown, no movement at all. The family didn't talk. Maybe, like Leo, they were wondering why they were here. Mum's job was the main reason, but Leo knew it was because of him too. If he had been more like other kids – more like Peg – none of this would have happened and they wouldn't have moved to this nowhere place.

THE POOL

The town pool, like everything in Dundle, was just a few minutes from the main street. It sat next to football fields and a cricket oval, and they were orangey-brown too. There was a scuffed-up tennis court, a square of bitumen for netball and a concrete skate ramp that looked like a wedge of space junk fallen from the sky.

Leo knew something was wrong straight-away. It was the hottest day he had ever known, the perfect day for a swim, and there was no one else around. They got out of the car and looked through the wire mesh fence at the pool.

Like the lagoon, it was empty. Not a single drop. It was another strange sight, like the school without children. Pools were supposed to be full of noise and laughter. Kids shrieking, water splashing, dive bombs and handstands; a sea of colour and life, and the smell of sunscreen and chlorine. Without water, it was just a concrete hole in the ground.

'Says here it's closed until …' Peg screwed up her face as she read a sign on the front gate. 'Closed until further notice. What does that mean?'

Dad guzzled from his water bottle. 'Not much. Just means it's closed until something else happens.'

'I'm sure it'll open again soon,' said Mum, pushing some extra brightness into her voice.

Before they went home, Leo stared at the empty pool and imagined it full of people. Saw himself jumping off the edge and kicking along the bottom, the cool water swallowing him up and washing away the heat. Then Dad beeped the car horn, making him jump and spin round. The others were in the car, engine running, waiting with weary faces. He ran and slid onto the back seat.

'Sorry.'

It was a small apology, but he wished it was bigger. He was sorry he always drifted off. He was sorry he couldn't make friends the way Peg did. And he was sorry they were here in Dundle, a dusty speck on the brown part of the map. He knew this place was wrong for him. He wouldn't find a friend or turn into Peg. But one other thing he definitely knew: he didn't want his parents to worry anymore.

As they drove home, he made sure not to imagine anything. No UFOs, no aliens bouncing on rooftops, no clouds above the town. And when he went to bed that night, he spied nothing strange or exciting in the sky. Just a crowd of ordinary stars.

SCHOOL

On the first day of school, Mum kissed everyone goodbye while they were still in bed.

'Love you, Leo,' she whispered. 'Have a great day and remember I'm proud of you.'

She didn't have far to go, but she had to get there early and stay late. Leo tried to go back to sleep. The room was already bright, so he pulled the sheet over his head. Squeezed his eyes shut and wished the morning would roll backwards into night.

'Today's the day!'

He threw back the sheet.

Peg stood at the door, already dressed in the Dundle school uniform. She even had her bag on her back. 'Come on. Get up!'

He closed his eyes and groaned.

☆

Dad walked with Leo and Peg to their classrooms. The school was small, but on that first day it was bustling with students, parents and teachers, all crisscrossing between the low buildings. There was a covered area with worn handball lines and a mural reminding everyone to be kind, but it wasn't much like his old school. He was used to hills and steps, and trees that shaded whole classroom blocks. This place looked like a few boxy buildings had landed on a flat dry paddock. The trees were tall and bony, there was more dirt than grass and he couldn't see any stairs at all.

As they moved through the school, he scanned the students. They were big, and not just because he was small. Their arms seemed thicker, their uniforms tight. Some kids were as tall as their parents. He and Dad said goodbye to Peg at her classroom and she joined a gaggle of Year 3 girls. Then he rounded a corner and came to the Year 4 room. A group of kids loafed around the door.

'Here we are.' Dad crouched so his face was level with Leo's. 'You okay?'

He wasn't okay. A jellyfish wobbled in the pit of his stomach. He could still taste toast in the back of his throat. But he didn't want Dad to worry, so he nodded.

'Okay. Remember your teacher's name?'

The jellyfish stirred. 'Ms Pengari.'

'Good. You'll be good. It'll be a good day.' Three goods. Maybe Dad was more nervous than he was. Still crouching, he put his hands on Leo's shoulders. 'Now, remember everything we've talked about. Tell me The Plan.'

The Plan was a list of ways that Leo could get to know other kids. His parents had talked through the list every night since they arrived in

Dundle and now Leo recited it all for his dad. *Ask about their holidays. Join an easy game like hide-and-seek. Find someone in the library and ask what they're reading.* There were lots of ideas and he counted them on his fingers.

They hugged and Dad smelt like coffee and soap. Then he said goodbye.

Leo's back sweated under the weight of his bag, stuffed with all the books he would need for the year. He slipped it off his shoulders and it hit the ground with a thud. The wobbly creature squirmed in his gut, and he dug his fingernails into his palms. For a moment, he allowed himself to look up, to take in the wide blue ceiling that had always calmed him. It looked so big, a bit like that day at the farm.

THUMP!

A soccer ball smacked into his stomach and knocked him over. He held his belly with both hands. Took some deep breaths. He could see the ball just out of reach. The name *Gus* was scrawled on one of its hexagons.

A huge boy galloped over and picked up the ball.

'Sorry, kid. Are you okay?'

Leo coughed. 'Yeah.'

The boy ran off with the ball.

The bell rang and Leo pushed himself up off the ground. He picked up his bag and kept holding his stomach. He was still a bit winded and it would hurt for a while, but at least it might keep that jellyfish quiet.

MS PENGARI

As Leo unloaded his books at the bag racks, the classroom door flew open. A woman stepped out, wearing a flowery Hawaiian shirt, fluoro yellow boardshorts and a pair of flippers. She had rainbow zinc striped across her face and wore a big floppy hat and sunglasses. Kids were still talking when she put a silver whistle to her mouth. The whistle shrieked and everyone went quiet. Then she took off her hat and sunglasses, and Leo saw a round, wide-eyed face with a beaming grin that could light up the night sky. Ms Pengari.

She eyed the jumble of kids, all silent and still.

'Goooood morning!' she sang. 'Year 4 is about to launch! You have two minutes to grab your gear, get in line and be ready to hop on board.'

Inside, the classroom was bright. At one end, a beach umbrella was surrounded by deck chairs, and pool toys hung from the ceiling: noodles, inflatable sharks and even a few boogie boards. Everyone found their desks and Leo looked around. It was a small class. There were some bigger boys in faded uniforms, a bunch of ponytailed girls who all looked the same, and a fidgety boy who tapped a pencil on his knee. It was a room full of kids he didn't know and a cold, familiar feeling wormed through his bones. Something from a long time ago. Not a jellyfish in his guts, but the shaky sense that he was suddenly five years old again, sitting on the edge of the colourful mat without a friend in the world.

Ms Pengari flip-flapped to the front of the

room in her flippers. She marked the roll and then put her hands on her hips.

'Who had fun at the pool in the holidays?'

No one moved, apart from a few kids who pulled confused faces. Even Leo knew this was a silly question.

'Exactly! No one had fun at the pool,' she said. 'That's why I'm dressed like this and I've brought all these pool things in – to remind you how much fun the pool can be.' She swept her arm at the inflatable creatures dangling from the ceiling. 'Look how much fun you should be having!'

A girl put up her hand. 'Isn't that a bit mean?'

Ms Pengari stroked her chin and nodded her zinc-smeared face. 'A little bit, yes. But I want you to do something about it.'

Leo leant forward. He had never known a teacher like this. She wouldn't have fit in at his old school. She probably didn't fit in at any school. But he couldn't look away as she explained her idea.

'We live in one of the hottest parts of the country and the Dundle pool has been closed for a year, all because there's not enough money to look after it.'

One of the bigger boys spoke up. 'Why do you need money for a pool? Just fill it with water and jump in.'

'Good question, Owen. Does anyone know? Why do we need money for a pool?'

Hands shot up in the air and a girl with straight black hair answered. 'You have to buy chemicals for the pool. And pay someone to put them in. Then maybe someone else to be in charge of it all and sell ice blocks and drinks.'

'Exactly,' said Ms Pengari. 'Plus, we'd have to find water from somewhere. Now, you all have the next few weeks to think of a way to raise some money. If the pool reopens, you can pull down these toys and have all the fun you should have had in the holidays.'

A wave of excited chatter washed round the room.

'But first,' she said, hands on hips, 'let's dive into the wonderful world of maths.'

The chatter died away as the children took their books from their desks.

BUDDIES

Leo didn't want to go to lunch. When everyone charged out of the classroom and pulled their lunchboxes from their bags, he stayed at his desk. If he went outside, he would have to put The Plan into place. He sat glued to his chair, stuck inside his Prep memories of kids butting in and walking away. He wanted to shrivel up, to find a hiding spot like the old office stairs. But the truth was he didn't want The Plan to work, and he didn't want to make friends. If he did, it would wreck the secret promise he had made with Ralph.

Ms Pengari sat on a chair next to him. 'Going okay, Leo?'

He spread his fingers out flat on the desk. 'Yeah.'

'Hope all this isn't too much. The pool stuff, my shirt, the warpaint on my face.'

'It's okay.'

She clasped her hands together. 'It must have been hard, saying goodbye to Ralph.'

He snapped her a look. 'What?'

'Your parents saw me last week. They told me about Ralph.'

He couldn't believe it. His whole body bristled. 'What did they say?'

'Not too much.' She took her time. Her hands were still and her eyes soft. 'They just said he was a great friend and that you had to say goodbye.'

He sat on his hands to stop them from shaking. Didn't know what to say.

Ms Pengari kept talking instead. 'The kids are friendly here at Dundle. But it might take a little while. You might not find anyone on the first day, or in the first week.'

This made Leo think of his promise with Ralph. The secret fizzed inside his chest.

'But I've organised something that might help.' She beckoned someone who must have been standing near the door. It was one of the other kids. A girl with short hair and a shiny lunchbox under her arm. 'This is Mia. She'll be your buddy at lunchtime today. And tomorrow you'll have a different buddy, and again the day after that – that way you can get to know different kids straightaway. Sound good?'

It sounded terrible. But he stood up, said thank you and left the room with Mia. He didn't want to do this, didn't want to do any of it – The Plan, the buddies, all this pretending – but he played along. He had his promise with Ralph to hold onto, and the other one he'd made with himself, to keep his parents from worrying.

THE TOWER

When school finished that day, Dad was waiting at the gate. He wanted to know everything, but Leo was tired and hot, so he bounced back short answers, like tapping a ping pong ball over a net. Soon, a swarm of kids arrived near the gate, one big group chatting and laughing. Peg was in the middle. All eyes were on her as she stopped, spread her arms wide and shouted the punchline to whatever story she was telling. The children burst into giggles, then funnelled through the gate with a chorus of 'Bye, Peg's and 'See you tomorrow's.

At home, Leo peeled off his hot school shirt and dunked his head under a cold shower for a full minute. He wolfed down a bowl of cereal and then they piled back into the car, with their bikes strapped on top. They drove to the empty lagoon and then Leo and Peg took off on their bikes, while Dad walked with a sketchbook in his hand and a pencil behind his ear.

Leo pedalled fast and the hot air hit his face like a hairdryer. Bugs skimmed off his helmet. Dead leaves on the path suddenly leapt to life as he whooshed past. He pushed the pedals harder and rode faster, so he could leave everything else behind: the jellyfish feeling, the shaky Prep memories, the lunchtime buddies his teacher had lined up. For a few minutes, he felt free of it all. Forgot he was even in Dundle. Then after a few laps, the big tower caught his eye and he skidded to a stop.

He sat on the bike with one foot on the ground. His chest rose and fell as he got his breath back and looked at the tower, about fifty metres away. There were two main parts – a big cylindrical body and a crisscrossed pattern of timber holding it up. The legs were giant stilts, with flights of wooden stairs zigzagging between them. They led to the top of the big metal body, where a balcony circled the tower, with a railing around the outside. Leo might not have cared about something like this in the city. But here, where everything was so dull and flat, the tower looked like something from another world, as if it had landed from space or was about to launch into orbit.

Peg caught up and stopped beside him. Then Dad arrived too. The three of them stood quietly for a while, looking at the tower. Flies found the backs of their shirts. A crow rattled from a gum tree.

'What is it?' Leo breathed normally, but his whole body was hot.

'A water tower,' said Dad. 'I guess they need them in places like this.'

‘I heard that it flooded here a long time ago,’ said Peg. ‘My teacher told me today.’

Leo used his shirt to wipe sweat from his face. He had imagined lots of things in his life, but he couldn’t picture Dundle under water. It was hard enough spotting a cloud.

‘If it’s full of water,’ said Peg, ‘why can’t they use it to grow some grass?’

‘Or fill the pool?’ said Leo.

Dad fanned his face with his hat. ‘They have to keep it for the important things: showers and baths, having enough to drink. Never know when it’ll rain again.’

Leo started pedalling back to the car, but he kept thinking about the tower. He imagined all the water inside and letting it out to soak the thirsty ground. Most of all, he thought about how big it was. He never expected to find something that tall in Dundle, as tall as a building in the city.

GUS

Leo's Monday buddy, Mia, didn't work out. She did what she had to do – showed him the toilets, the drink bubblers and the tuckshop – but then she left him alone in the eating area and sat with her friends. He didn't mind and didn't tell anyone about it. He wanted to get through the week without making people worry.

On Tuesday, he was told to stick with Finn at lunchtime – a mousy kid who took two bites of a sandwich and then ran to the library. Leo followed and found him playing a complicated card game with a group of boys. They were all hunched around a table, snapping and flinging the cards and calling out words he had never heard before.

'Volta!'

'Shuck!'

'Double dink!'

Leo backed away. He dropped himself into a beanbag and thumbed through a book he didn't want to read.

Wednesday and Thursday weren't any better: a clumsy attempt at handball with a boy called Rafi, and half an hour listening to Nicola talk about her horse. A few times, Leo tried to speak, but his sentences fell out in stuttered spurts and the buddies didn't listen. Both days left him deflated. He knew they were doing their duty for Ms Pengari, and nothing more.

The nervous Prep feeling didn't drown him for the rest of the week, but it was always there, lapping at the edges. He tried a few things from The Plan, so he could tell Mum and Dad he had given it a go. As the weekend neared, he thought less about school and focused on his secret promise with Ralph. On the night he said goodbye, the promise had glimmered like a distant star inside his mind. Now it began to shine brighter, like a burning comet getting closer each day. By Friday, it was almost all he could think about.

His last buddy for the week was the biggest boy in the class. His name was Gus, and Leo recognised him from the first day, when the soccer ball had pummelled into his stomach. Gus was a bulky kid, as if his body was built from chunks of wood. His arms were like branches and his legs like trunks. At lunchtime on Friday, they ate on a bench seat, and Gus talked about the ball as he rolled it back and forth under his foot.

'My dad gave me this ball for my birthday, years ago.' His voice was softer than Leo expected. 'I haven't seen Dad in ages, so I keep it with me all the time.'

Leo had seen the ball trapped under Gus's foot in class. He hadn't thought about it much until now.

'Most kids around here play footy. They want me to play too because I'm big. But I love soccer. One day I'm gonna move to the city and play for one of the big clubs.'

Leo peeled a mandarin. He hadn't expected to hear this kid's life story, hadn't expected to care, but something about Gus's quiet voice drew him in. He ran through The Plan in his head, searching for a question that might fit here. But Gus got in first.

'What kind of things are you into?'

It wasn't the question that caught Leo out. It was the pause that came afterwards. He wasn't used to kids giving him time to talk and he found himself answering honestly.

'I like ... space.' He waited to be interrupted, but it didn't happen. 'And I like aliens. Lots of people don't think they're real, but I do.'

Gus didn't say anything. He didn't walk

away, either, but Leo assumed he'd wandered off in his head. Probably thinking about running to the oval and belting his ball into the goal. They didn't talk for the rest of the day until the final bell. Leo was at the bag racks, zipping up his backpack when he heard Gus muttering to himself. There was panic in his voice.

'No, no, no.' He lifted bags and swept hats aside. 'Where is it?' He tipped everything out of his own backpack. Pencils and scrunched paper fell on the ground. 'No!'

Leo stood still with his bag on his back. Everyone else had gone. 'Are you—'

'My ball!' Gus pushed past him and hunted through a scraggly garden bed outside the room. 'It's gone!'

'Do you remember, you know, where you last—'

Gus climbed onto a table and stood on his toes, trying to see on top of the classroom roof. Then he cupped his hands around his mouth and yelled, 'Who took my ball?!'

He jumped down and staggered back to the bag racks.

Leo hadn't moved. 'Do you, er, want some help?'

Gus didn't answer. He scooped his things back into his bag and ran off. His shoes smacked the concrete like claps of thunder and Leo was left alone, like a small tree that had survived a storm. He knew the hurt of losing something precious. That's why he'd tried to help. But Gus, like so many other kids, had ignored him.

It didn't matter anyway. He didn't need a friend. The week had almost passed and soon he could forget about lunchtime buddies and Mum and Dad's plan. His promise with Ralph would fix everything.

THE SECRET

Saturday dragged and Sunday meandered, but by the late afternoon, as the weekend neared its end, Leo was itchy with excitement. He walked aimless circles in the backyard and ran up and down the steps for no reason. He finally settled on the verandah just before dinner and marvelled at the Dundle sky. It was the biggest part of the picture. At Leo's old place near the city, the sky looked like an afterthought, the last thing to be coloured once all the buildings and roads and trees were in place. Here, it filled his eyes more than anything else. As they ate dinner, the sun dipped behind the rooftops and that enormous blue sky started to fade, then grow dark. A bunch of galahs squawked from a powerline and, at the table, Peg talked about school.

'I can't wait to see Imogen and Bree tomorrow.'

Dad scooped lasagne onto his plate. 'They're your friends?'

'Yep,' she said. 'And another girl, Greta.'

Mum forked some salad from a bowl and talked about her job: parent meetings and teenage fights and looking after new teachers. It sounded horrible to Leo, but Mum's hands danced around, and her face was so happy. Then Dad took over and showed them some of his pictures, sketchbooks filled with windmills and fenceposts, shopfronts, road signs and cars. After only a week, everyone except Leo had found their place in Dundle.

They stopped talking for a while. Cutlery scraped. A frog croaked. Then Mum turned to Leo.

'What about you?'

He swallowed. 'Me?'

'Are you looking forward to seeing Imogen and Bree too?' She faked a smile to go with the joke.

He shrugged and played along. 'Yeah, I can't wait.'

It was half the truth – he couldn't wait for tomorrow – but there was a heavy secret hidden underneath. He was looking forward to everything because of the promise he'd made with Ralph, and the promise was this: if he hadn't made a friend after one week at school, Ralph would find him in Dundle and they would be together again. When they made the promise, Ralph had hesitated.

'One week isn't very long,' he'd said.

Leo threw his arms wide. 'It's ages!'

'But won't your parents—'

'They won't find out,' Leo had said. 'Not if we're careful.'

Now, as he leant back in his chair and

watched the stars blinking in the Dundle sky, his legs jiggled under the table and the jellyfish twirled in his belly. He hadn't tried very hard to make friends. He hadn't really bothered with The Plan or the buddies. He'd resisted it all for the promise with Ralph and when tomorrow came, he would be with his friend again.

AN EMPTY SKY

Leo woke early, before the sun lit up his room. He opened the curtains, pressed his face to the window and looked up. The sky was half-asleep, dreaming of a colour between black and dawn blue. Any moment now, the white balloon would swing into view and Ralph would be holding on.

But he never came. Leo waited by the window until Mum said her early goodbye, then he raced out to the yard and spun round, trying to scan the whole sky at once. Still no Ralph. He started to sweat. His throat dried up. Maybe Ralph would meet him at school.

With bags on backs, he and Peg rolled their bikes down the driveway and turned onto the road. Dad was with them, pedalling a cobwebbed mountain bike he had hardly used. The streets were wide, like flat grey rivers lined with tired trees. Every surface was sapped by the sun, and even the houses and street signs seemed to lean in the heat. Leo kept his eyes up, searching for a white dot on that big canvas of blue. But he had never seen anything so empty.

They parked their bikes in the racks at school.

Dad hugged them. 'You'll be okay riding home by yourselves?'

'Yep,' said Peg, unclipping her helmet.

'Yeah,' said Leo, looking up.

They walked to their classrooms and Leo tripped a few times as he tipped his head back, scanning for Ralph.

'Who's that kid?' whispered Peg. 'He was just looking at you.'

He turned from the sky. The big shape of Gus wandered towards their classroom.

'That's Gus.' Leo looked back up at the sky. 'All he talks about is—'

Soccer. That was what he was going to say. But when he glanced again at Gus, his whole body was hunched and there was no ball at his feet. It was still missing. The thing he cared about more than anything in the world wasn't there. Leo knew how that felt.

'He's huge,' Peg said. 'Are you friends?'

'No.' The answer came out faster than Leo expected.

☆

He spent the day staring out the window and listening for a thump on the side of the classroom. The other kids paired up to talk about ideas for the pool, but Leo stayed at his desk, scribbling a picture of Ralph. When everyone else ran out to lunch, Ms Pengari asked him to wait. She wore a black witch's hat and carried a plastic wand, ready for the next lesson about the magic of measurement.

'Hang in there,' she said. 'The first week at a new school is always hard. And Dundle's different from the city. It must feel like another planet.'

Leo scratched his leg with his other foot. Another planet sounded like a good idea.

She propped her witch's hat higher on her head. 'How did you go with the buddies last week?'

'There's – well – not really anyone I could – could be friends with.' His words were limping out. He faced the carpet.

'You mean, there's no one like Ralph?'

His eyes flicked up.

'There's nothing wrong with feeling like you don't fit. Look at me!' She should have been scary with the hat and black lipstick, but there was too much kindness in her face. 'It won't be long till someone likes the way you don't fit.'

There was only one friend like that – and he was supposed to be floating into town right now. Leo had to get outside to check. He drifted to the eating area and lay on a seat so he could see nothing but sky. A noisy handball game bounced around nearby. A small voice asked what he was doing, but he didn't answer. Everything sounded far away, like he had fallen under water.

THE TREE

Ralph didn't turn up at school that day. Not in the sky, not in the classroom and not at the bike racks when it was home time. Leo and Peg started riding home together, but she sped on ahead with some friends.

'See you at home!' she sang over her shoulder.

He pedalled along the edge of the gutter and replayed the promise in his mind. A week had passed. He hadn't made any friends. Ralph was supposed to be here.

He gave up on the sky and watched the bike tyre spinning slowly. A soft breeze, the first he'd felt in Dundle, tickled the back of his neck. Then a grey feather swooped past his face. It flipped and twirled and climbed higher until it got stuck in a tree. Leo stopped. There was something further up in the tree, round and white. It looked like a balloon.

He jumped off his bike and ran to the tree. It shaded a wooden bench seat and a water tap – the smallest park in the world. He circled the trunk, head tilted back, trying to spot the balloon through the mess of limbs and leaves. It was there, right at the top. This was just like the day Ralph had first arrived. Leo stepped up onto the seat and stretched for the lowest branch. It was just out of reach, so he jumped, gripped it with both hands and hung there for a few seconds. Then he pulled himself up so he was crouching on the branch, and kept on going, clambering up through the arms of the tree. As he climbed higher and the ground fell away, his heart drummed louder and his legs trembled. He was nearly at the balloon and maybe Ralph would be there too, nestled at the top of the tree, waiting for Leo to find him.

At last, the round white shape was almost in reach. He lifted himself up one more branch and there it was. Round and white – but not what he expected. It was too round, too dirty and not a balloon at all. It was a soccer ball and it had Gus's name on it.

The effort of the climb suddenly caught up with him. A groan choked in the back of his throat. He sucked deep breaths and his chest burned as if he'd swallowed the sun. Cicadas rattled. A cockatoo screeched. The tree seemed to sway like it wanted to shake him off and the whole town wobbled below.

He shut his eyes and filled his lungs with air. His heart slowed and the dizziness lifted, but he couldn't work out what had happened. He thought it was the balloon, thought he had found Ralph. But it was just a soccer ball and now he'd be late home. Dad would fire a hundred questions at him. He'd frown and scratch the back of his head and blame it all on Ralph. Then all the grown-ups would worry again and they'd move somewhere worse than Dundle.

Leo buried his head in his hands. 'Where are you, Ralph?' He needed him more than ever.

TRUTH AND LIES

Dad was pacing the footpath when Leo got home. He wasn't just frowning and scratching – he was tugging at his hair and his face was red.

'Where have you been?'

Leo slowed the bike to a shaky stop. It was hard to ride while holding a soccer ball. He had steered with one hand the whole way home.

Dad pointed at the ball. 'Is that why you're late?'

Leo looked at it tucked under his arm. 'Yeah.'

'But you don't like soccer.'

'Well, I'm not very good.'

He was telling truth and lies at the same time.

'And whose is it?'

Leo remembered the name on the ball. 'It's Gus's. He's a kid in my class.'

'So why do you have it?'

Leo could feel himself getting trapped. He read Gus's name again and thought of him slouching through the day without his favourite thing in the world. 'Well – I'm looking after it for tonight. I'll give it back tomorrow.'

It was another lie wrapped in a truth, but it seemed to work. Dad stopped asking questions. The fire in his face went out. 'So there's nothing else I need to know?' He shot a look at Leo's hand. His pinky finger was tucked away.

Leo shook his head. 'Just that I'm sorry. I didn't mean to be late.'

Only the truth this time. Dad gave him a hug and Leo pushed his bike under the house.

THUMP

There was a box in Leo's room that he hadn't unpacked. That night, he lifted it onto his desk and peeled off the tape. The first thing he pulled out was his space lamp. When it was switched on, it threw stars all over a darkened room. Next was the pile of coloured stones he used to play Asteroids. There were a few space books and a poster of the planets. And finally his album of alien friends.

On the opening page was the Gronk, the first playdough alien he'd made. He smiled at his crooked Prep writing. Then there was a Fump, a Wozzle and a Meeb. He turned the pages and remembered each alien until he stopped at a picture that didn't match the others. It was the photo he'd taken on the morning he met Ralph, the shot of the messy bed. Ralph hadn't materialised in the printed picture, but Leo had glued it in the book anyway. Just because you couldn't see something, didn't mean it wasn't there.

He touched the photo. 'Tomorrow you see.'

He didn't really know what tomorrow would bring. And he had never felt more alone. All the days in front of him were as blank as an empty sky.

He put the album back in the box, opened the curtains and climbed into bed. But he was so tired the stars blurred into fuzzy white spots. He closed his eyes and sank into a sleep so dreamless and deep that he almost didn't hear the thump on the wall outside his room.

He opened one eye. His heartbeat throbbed in his head. Then he sat up and watched a short, furry shape fumble through the window and hit the floor. The stumpy silhouette stood up, brushed itself off and then stepped into the square of moonlight that fell into the room.

'Ralph?' Leo's voice shook. 'It's really you?'

Ralph flapped his ears and wiggled his horns. His eyes shone. 'Sorry I'm late.'

Leo threw the blankets aside and wrapped his arms around his friend, nearly knocking him over. His fur was soft and it shimmered.

'I still need you,' Leo said.

'I know.' Ralph hugged him tight.

THE BALL

For weeks, Leo had kept his promise a secret. Now he had to keep *Ralph* a secret and it started as soon as the sun lit up his room.

'Bye, love.' Mum gave him a kiss as he yawned awake. 'Anything big happening today?'

He stretched. Rubbed his eyes. Felt his furry friend snuggle beside him. 'Not really – just a normal day.'

'Okay, love you.'

He listened as her shoes clicked out the door, down the steps, then he peeked out the window and watched her walk across the patchy field towards the high school buildings. Ralph was slow to wake. Leo tickled his flappy ears. Ralph swatted his hand away, rolled over and started snoring again. Leo poked his mushroom nose.

'Hey!' Ralph sat up this time. 'What's wrong?'

Leo bounded out of bed and stretched his arms out wide. 'You're here – nothing's wrong!'

As he got ready for school, he told Ralph everything about Dundle. The dry lagoon. The empty pool. Ms Pengari and all her costumes. When he mentioned the tower, Ralph stopped him.

'Wait – tell me about the tower.' His fur was the colour of warm custard.

'It's huge,' said Leo. 'Bigger than anything else in the town. And there are stairs that go up through the middle.'

'All the way to the top?'

'Yeah. Why?'

Ralph's horns stood straight and his ears fluttered. 'Oh, nothing.' He spread his paws out wide, like Leo had. 'Let's go to school!'

Leo threw his bag on his back and grabbed the soccer ball from his wardrobe.

'Is that for Gus?' said Ralph.

'Yeah.'

Leo had told him about the ball in the tree, but he hadn't talked about Gus. Ralph might have read the name on the ball. Or perhaps he just knew, the way he knew which window to climb in last night. Leo didn't think hard about it. He had his friend again, his most important thing in the world. It felt like a missing puzzle piece was locked back into place and it was time to give Gus his own missing piece.

THE KICK

When Leo walked to his classroom that morning, he held his head a bit higher and added a skip between his steps. He didn't need a lunchtime buddy. Had no need for Mum and Dad's lists. None of that mattered anymore because Ralph was right there, trotting beside him, a shade of buttery gold.

He found Gus before class, standing on the dusty oval. He looked lost, a statue in a school shirt, like he was waiting for his ball to fall from the sky.

Ralph squeezed Leo's finger. 'Call out to him.'

Leo held the ball in his other hand. 'Really?'

His friend pushed him in the back. 'Go on.'

Leo took a few steps onto the oval. 'Gus! Over here!'

Gus turned.

Leo held the ball high. 'It's yours!' He was better at yelling than he thought.

Gus came closer and called back, 'Really?'

'Yeah.'

A toothy smile spread across Gus's face. He leapt and did an awkward dance in the dirt. He was too big to do any of it gracefully, but he didn't seem to care. 'You're the best!' He started to run to Leo then stopped. 'Hey – kick it from there.'

Leo scrunched his nose. 'What?'

'Kick it!'

Leo had never kicked a ball properly in his life. He always missed and landed on his back, or stood on the ball and fell on his face.

'Kick it.'

It wasn't Gus's voice. It was Ralph's. He

waggled his horns and hopped from foot to foot. 'You can do it.'

Maybe Ralph was right. Maybe he could do it. He held the ball with both hands, straight out in front. He narrowed his eyes, focused on the ball and took a few strides. In one quick movement, he dropped the ball and prodded his leg forward. He could see in his mind what was supposed to happen. The ball would hurtle through the air in a perfect curve and land at Gus's feet. But he missed. His leg flew past the ball, his other foot skidded in the dirt, and he clattered to the ground in a jumble of limbs.

Gus ran over and lifted him up with one hand. 'Are you okay?'

Leo clapped dirt off his shirt and shorts. Tears pricked his eyes.

'Thanks again for finding my ball,' said Gus. 'I can't believe it.'

Leo rubbed a grazed elbow. 'It was at the top of a tree.'

'What – did you climb up and get it?'

'Yeah.' He didn't say why – that he'd thought it was a balloon from space.

'Wow. Thanks.'

Gus strode off, dribbling the ball with his feet. Leo straightened the bag on his back and Ralph held his finger as they walked to class.

When his elbow stopped stinging, and the embarrassment wore off, Leo scowled at his friend. 'Can't believe you made me kick a ball.'

'Sorry,' said Ralph. 'But it looked pretty funny.' His fur turned cheeky orange.

THE ART ROOM

Ms Pengari marched around the room, dressed as a lifeguard: red-and-yellow cap, whistle round her neck and a pair of pineapple sunglasses covering half her face.

Ralph leant in close to Leo. 'She reminds me of some aliens I know, from the planet Quon.'

The teacher moved between the desks and talked about the Dundle pool. 'You've had a week to come up with ideas. I want to know how we can raise some money so we can go swimming again.' She swept an arm towards the inflatable toys, still hanging from the ceiling. 'These poor creatures must be returned to their natural habitat – a swimming pool full of noisy kids.'

Suggestions came from around the room. Some children wanted to sell biscuits. Others wanted a fun run. Leo hadn't thought much about it. With Ralph by his side, he was keen to explore the night sky again, but he didn't see how that could raise any money.

Halfway through the lesson, there was a loud bang from the side of the room. The children jumped in their seats and turned around. The noise had come from the air-con unit, an old box-shaped thing that chugged from behind the teacher's desk, but had now started to splutter and cough. It banged again, hissed like a punctured tyre and went quiet.

'Well, that's broken,' said one of the boys.

Ms Pengari wasted no time. 'We can't stay here,' she said. 'We'll roast.' She looked out the window, back at the students, then grabbed a jangle of keys from her desk drawer. 'Hats on, everyone. Let's go.'

Ralph skipped beside Leo as the class followed Ms Pengari to a small building near the back fence. She unlocked the door, switched on the air-con and invited everyone in. There were paint-spattered benches, sinks along the walls, and shelves stacked with art gear: brushes, crayons, pencils and pens. Leo sat on a plastic stool and Ralph climbed onto his knee.

Ms Pengari took off her pineapple sunglasses. 'The good news is the air-con works. The other good news is we didn't bring our books, so we'll have some free art time.'

The children cheered and gathered supplies from the cupboards and shelves. Some kids tipped paint into cups and others grabbed wire and blocks of styrofoam. Leo used fishing line to slice off a lump of damp clay. He broke it into smaller chunks and rolled them into perfect spheres.

Ralph sat on the bench. 'What are you making?'

Leo kept his voice low. 'The planets.'

'And the moons?'

'Not all of them. Maybe just Ralphora.'

It had been a while since Leo had talked like this and he wanted to dive back into his old games.

'Hey, Ralph. We should play Asteroids when we get home.'

Ralph looked away. 'Maybe.'

'What about Other Worlds? We could play it from the verandah.'

Ralph's fur was a dull beige. Not the yellow Leo expected. 'Not much fun without a telescope.'

Leo winced at the memory of their big goodbye, when he had thrown the telescope in the bin.

'What are you making?'

Leo bunched his eyebrows. 'I already told you.'

'Huh?'

Leo froze. It wasn't Ralph talking this time. It was Gus, sitting on his other side. He kept rolling the clay. 'I'm – making some planets.'

Gus inspected the spheres. 'I don't know much about space. What do you like about it?'

This huge kid had a way of asking questions that Leo wanted to answer, like he was offering a perfect peach you just had to bite into.

'That's – well, that's what I like. That we don't know much about it. It's mysterious and we've still got lots to find out.' He returned the question. 'What are you making?'

Gus hunched, like he wanted to make himself smaller. 'Oh, just me and my dad. Playing soccer.'

They were quiet for a while. Leo shaped his planets. Gus made some soccer goals. Ralph practised handstands at the side of the room.

Then Gus tossed a question that Leo didn't want to touch. 'Who's Ralph?'

'What?'

'Ralph. I heard you say something about Ralph before.'

The ball of clay slipped from Leo's fingers

and landed on the table. 'He's – he's a friend from my old school.'

He waited for Gus's curiosity to fade, like sitting out a storm. He busied himself with another blob of clay, rolling it against the surface of the bench. After a few mindless minutes, he held in his hands a smooth cylinder. He stood it on one end and made a bunch of tall legs to hold it up. It was the strange tower near the lagoon. Ralph was suddenly beside him, staring at the miniature tower. His fur washed lemon-yellow and he didn't look away.

THE BARBECUE

A few days later, Leo waited with his family on the footpath outside a tall wooden house. His hair was slicked back and he wore a collared shirt tucked into long pants. As he tightened then loosened his belt, a streetlight blinked on and coated them all with an orange glow.

'What's this all about again?' Dad lifted an esky of drinks from the boot of the car.

'I told you.' Mum took a pencil from behind his ear. 'Every year Mr Oliver hosts a welcome back barbecue for all the high school teachers.'

Peg fussed with her headband. 'Who's Mr Oliver?'

'He's the principal. My boss.' Mum pulled her stern teacher face. 'So you all have to behave yourselves. Especially you.' She pointed a finger at Dad's chest and kissed him on the cheek.

Leo pulled a face. Ralph went cross-eyed. 'You be good too,' Leo whispered as they walked through the gate.

'Wow!' Peg's mouth dropped open. 'Look at this place!'

Cushions and blankets were spilt across the grass. Small lanterns nestled in the forks of trees and fairy lights zigzagged above their heads like a ceiling of stars. There were tables spread with cheese and dips, the smell of barbecued sausages wafted in the air, and jangly country music blared from a pair of speakers.

Leo and Peg followed Mum's orders and said hello to Mr Oliver. He was a lean man with a friendly face that bent forward, so he seemed interested all the time.

'Nice to meet you, kids.' He leant towards Leo and shook his hand.

Then they were free. For Peg, that meant bouncing up to every other teacher's kid who came through the gate, linking arms and inventing games. Leo piled a plate with mini sausage rolls and sat under a lantern in the corner of the yard, next to a pool fence. Ralph did somersaults on the grass.

'Hey, Ralph.' He bit into a sausage roll. 'What should we do to help the town pool? I want to do something about space.'

Ralph sat up and frowned. 'What's so good about the town pool?'

'What do you mean?'

Ralph stood. 'There's a perfectly good pool right there.' He was orange all over and there was a cheeky smirk on his face.

Leo had seen that look before. 'Ralph? What are you doing?'

He didn't answer. Just edged closer to the pool fence.

'Ralph?'

He stuck an arm through the fence, then a leg.

'Ralph – don't.'

His whole body wriggled through and he was suddenly at the pool's edge, grinning.

'What are you doing?' Leo couldn't hide the bubble of delight in his voice. 'You can't go swimming now.'

Ralph poked a hairy foot at the water and nearly dunked it in. He giggled and pulled it back. Then he tiptoed along the edge of the pool, arms out wide, like a tightrope walker. He swayed left and right, threatening to overbalance and fall in.

'Not funny, Ralph!'

Leo didn't mean it – it was hilarious. Ralph skipped and bopped all around the pool. Pretended to dive in, wiggled some wonky dance moves and shook his body like he was covered in cockroaches. He was a scruffy whirlwind of silliness, spinning and twirling until Leo collapsed against the pool fence, out of breath with laughter.

'Leo, what are you doing?' Mum was holding a glass of punch. Her head was tilted to the side like she was trying to solve a puzzle. 'Were you talking to someone?'

Leo tried to flatten his crumpled shirt and get his breath back. 'It was just a bit noisy,' he said, still puffing. 'So I sat over here.'

She narrowed her eyes. Scanned either side of him like she was hunting for the real answer. 'Well, I think you should come back.'

She rejoined the crowd. He sighed.

Ralph squeezed back through the fence. 'Do you think she knows I'm here?'

'Where?'

'Here,' said Ralph. 'In Dundle.'

Leo never struggled talking to Ralph. Words came out easily. But this time, he didn't know what to say.

IMPORTANT STUFF

On Saturday, Leo rode his bike like a bullet round the lagoon. The sun was barely awake but already blinding and bright, as if it had never slept. Cockatoos dotted the trees, kangaroos chewed tufts of grass, and clouds of yellow butterflies swept all around. Leo pedalled hard and laughed even harder. Laughed because he couldn't help it, because it was a beautiful day, but mostly because his best friend Ralph was right there with him, clinging on like a furry backpack.

As he zoomed around for another lap, Mum,

Dad and Peg set up a barbecue breakfast in the nearby park. It was a big circuit and he was mostly out of their sight, which made it easier to talk to Ralph.

'Am I going too fast?'

'Never!'

'Wanna go faster?'

'Yes!'

Leo pumped his legs harder. The pedals spun in blurry circles. Ducks flapped off the path and dragonflies veered out of the way. Ralph's sun-kissed fur danced in the wind and Leo felt the warmth of it against his neck. His big mushroom nose drank in the morning air right next to Leo's face.

'Stop!' Ralph pointed a hairy paw. He had spotted the tower.

Leo stopped the bike. He felt something shift in Ralph.

'I want a closer look,' his friend said.

Leo steered off the path and bumped the bike along the dirt. He pedalled into the tower's shadow, slowed down and looked up. It was even bigger up close. Birds wheeled around the roof, clouds floated past, and it seemed everything was moving except the tower, like the whole world was spinning around this bulging metal tank.

Leo took his feet off the pedals and planted them on the ground. Ralph slid off his back and stood at the wire fence that bordered the tower.

'Dad said it's for holding water,' said Leo. 'But not for plants or the pool. More important stuff.'

Ralph's ears lifted. His fur was yellow. 'Yeah, important stuff.'

Leo rested his bike on the ground and crouched next to his friend, staring up. 'Are you okay?'

Ralph blinked. 'Yeah. I'm glad I saw it.' Then he shook himself like he was waking from a dream. 'Let's get back to breakfast.'

He turned and waited next to the bike. Leo picked it up, hopped on and started pedalling.

Ralph ran alongside, then threw himself onto Leo's back, like he was jumping onto a moving train. They rode out of the tower's shadow and around the dry lagoon. By the time they reached the family, Ralph's fur was as bright as it had ever been.

GLOOPS

There were no office stairs in Dundle State School, but Leo and Ralph found a cosy spot next to the library. It was a square of pavers hidden behind an overgrown shrub where the sun couldn't hit them. A space that was cool, quiet and just big enough for two friends to huddle at lunchtime.

Leo peeled a banana. Ralph sat still beside him. His fur had been weak yellow all day – happy, but faraway.

'What are you thinking about?' Leo said.

Ralph blinked his watery eyes. 'Just

something from Ralphora. We had this food, a bit like fruit, that would grow on small trees. It was shaped like half a moon.'

'What did it taste like?'

'A banana and an apple at the same time. We called them gloops.'

'Gloops?' Leo looked at the banana in his hand. 'They should be called – banapples!'

Leo laughed, but Ralph still seemed somewhere else.

'Do you miss it? Not the gloops, I mean – Ralphora.'

Ralph gave something like a shrug – it was hard to tell because he barely had shoulders. Leo chomped his banana and looked at the cloudless sky. Then Gus walked past, holding his lunchbox.

Ralph suddenly jumped to his feet and shoved Leo in the back. 'Say hi.'

Leo shook him off. 'What?'

'Say hi to that Gus kid.'

'Why?'

'Just do it.'

Leo half-stood. 'Hey, hi.' He waved.

Gus turned back. He had the soccer ball at his feet. 'Hi.'

Leo scrambled for the next thing to say. 'Um, do you want to sit here?'

Gus rolled the ball, side to side, under his foot. 'Okay.'

Leo moved over to give him room. A shade of warm honey washed over Ralph's fur.

Gus opened his lunchbox and ripped the sticker off an apple. 'When you kicked the ball the other day – guess you haven't played much soccer.' It would have sounded mean in anyone else's voice but not the way Gus said it. 'What did you play at your old school? I mean, with Ralph?'

Leo ate some more banana. 'Oh – just space stuff.'

'Did you make the games up yourself?'

'Yeah.'

'Like what?'

Gus left so much room for thinking, and Leo took his time. He remembered straightaway the games he had invented, but he was suddenly scared to name them out loud. What would this big soccer kid think of Bounce the Moon and Asteroids? And why did he care anyway?

'Doesn't matter,' he said. 'I don't play them anymore.'

Gus bit a chunk of apple. 'Well, I think it's cool you made up your own games. I couldn't do that.'

Ralph's fur was still honey-coloured and he gave Leo a nudge. 'Tell him about Other Worlds.'

Leo was confused. Last time he mentioned Other Worlds, Ralph turned beige and whinged about the broken telescope.

Now he was flapping his ears and wiggling his horns. 'Go on.'

Leo took a breath. 'There was a game called Other Worlds. We'd find stars in the sky and imagine they were planets. We made up aliens and gave them silly names.'

'Like what?'

'One was a Gronk.'

'A Gronk?' Gus grinned.

'And one was called a Wozzle.'

Gus laughed and some apple flew out of his mouth.

Leo laughed too, but kept going. 'Bollybops. Dinkles. Some were called Fumps.'

Gus's whole body shook with laughter. His face turned red.

'But my favourite aliens were Grimbles. They had two heads and talked backwards.'

Gus was rolling around laughing, holding his belly with one hand and the soccer ball with the other. When he finally sat up, his eyes were still watering. 'Talk backwards? How do you do it?'

'Okay,' said Leo. 'I'll ask you a question: soccer like you do why?'

Gus's face was blank. 'What does that mean?'

'Why do you like soccer? But I said it backwards.'

'Oh. Okay.' Gus twisted his face. 'Because … fun … is … I can't do it.'

Leo shrugged and closed his lunchbox. He shouldn't have tried. 'We used to play Other Worlds with a telescope, but it broke, so I threw it away.'

'A telescope?' Gus crunched into his apple. 'Those big things you look through at night?'

'Yeah.'

Gus swallowed. 'I think there's one in our house, but I've never used it. It's under of pile of stuff in Mum's sewing room.' The image hung between them while he finished his apple. When he spoke again, his words stumbled, the way Leo sometimes talked. 'Do you, ah, wanna check it out – one day?'

Leo wasn't sure how this had happened. He had Ralph and he didn't need anyone else. But he liked the idea of looking through a telescope again, especially one that didn't have a cracked lens. He missed seeing the moon and stars up close.

'Okay. I mean – sure.'

Gus stood up. 'Okay, then. See ya.' He jumped the shrubs and ran to the oval with his ball.

Leo scrunched his eyes shut and opened them again. The last few minutes whirled in his head. He held out his pinky finger, but Ralph wasn't there. He spun around, looked under the hedge and around the corner of the library. Then he saw him, swinging his legs on a low branch, the colour of a golden dawn. He flapped his ears and waved.

Leo waved back and spoke under his breath. 'What are you so happy about?'

THE MOON

Gus's place was a small brick house with a rambly garden. Plants climbed fenceposts and overflowed onto the front path. A rusty wheelbarrow, full of yellow flowers, leant against a tree.

Dad drummed his fingers on the steering wheel. 'It's been five minutes. Should we go in? I'm not sure how long we can sit in a parked car before it starts looking suspicious.'

'Probably ten minutes,' said Peg. 'Someone'll call the police after that.'

'Don't be silly,' Mum said from the front

seat. 'No one's calling the police. And Leo can take as long as he wants.'

Leo stared at the house. All of this was unexpected. He never thought he'd visit Gus and he certainly didn't want the whole family to come along. Then there was Ralph. His fur was mango gold, and he pressed his mushroom nose against the window, trembling with excitement. All week, he had talked about the telescope. He wanted to see it. *Had* to see it.

At last, they all unfolded themselves from the car and were soon inside, buried in hugs from Gus's mum and grandma. They were both short women, had wavy black hair and the sunniest faces Leo had ever seen. They talked at the same time, like overlapping melodies.

'I hope you like it here in—'

'Dundle is a lovely place to—'

'Raise a family and—'

'It's got everything you need and—'

'Everyone's so friendly.'

The first ten minutes were a cheerful blur.

Gus's mum and grandma made cups of tea, asked questions and then told each other to stop asking questions. They hardly took a breath, but were so much fun that no one seemed to mind. It was like being wrapped in a warm blanket of words.

Gus pulled Leo away from the others. Ralph skipped along with them, clutching Leo's finger. They moved around the house and Gus pointed out some photos. An action shot of him playing soccer. Another of him riding a horse. Then a small framed photo of him and his dad, both with a ball trapped under a foot. After a few minutes, they came to the biggest room in the house. Two sewing machines sat on a long table, and all around were half-dressed mannequins, scraps of material, furry coats, felt hats and rolls and rolls of ribbon. It was a colourful mess, as if someone had thrown everything into the room, shaken it up like a cup of dice, and let each thing find its own place.

'Mum and Grandma make clothes,' Gus said. 'This is their sewing room, but the telescope's in here too.'

There was a pile of sheets draped over something near the window. Gus lifted them and underneath was the telescope. But it was nothing like the plastic tube Leo had owned. It was beautiful. Almost as big as Gus, made of shiny metal, and cradled in a tripod carved from thick timber. Leo circled it, marvelling at the eyepiece, the dials, the jingly chain hanging from the lens cover. There were other parts too, that Leo didn't recognise. Clamps and knobs and an extra mini scope. It looked like something from a museum, or from the deck of an ancient ship.

Gus tapped the main tube. 'It's my dad's. He used it a lot, a long time ago. Now it just sits in here, buried under stuff.'

Leo touched one of the timber legs. 'Have you ever looked through it?'

Gus shrugged. 'I didn't want to break it. But we can try.'

Leo unscrewed the lens cap and Gus used a strip of material to clean the glass. Then Leo swivelled the telescope and angled it at the sky. It was daytime so there wasn't much to find until Gus pointed in another direction. The moon had crept into sight. It hung there in the empty blue, like an overnight guest who had forgotten to go home. Leo swung the telescope gently, peered through the eyepiece and focused the lens. Straightaway, the moon filled his view. A bright, powdery half-circle, pocked with craters and empty seabeds. Through the old telescope, it was as crisp as a photograph. A small wave of joy coursed through his body. Goosebumps pimpled his arms. It was like being up close with an old friend.

Gus had a turn. He had to bend a bit further and it took him a moment to look through the eyepiece at the right angle. Then everything must have lined up because he stayed completely still. 'Wow. It's like I'm seeing it for the first time.' He stood like that, hunched and unmoving, for a few minutes. 'I could look at the moon every night, and Dad could look at it too. We'd be in different places, but we'd be seeing the same thing at the same time.' Then he stepped back from the telescope and fixed Leo with startled eyes. 'But sometimes the moon disappears. What would I do then?'

Leo thought for a while. Gus always gave him time to think. At last, he knew just what to say. 'Just because you can't see something, doesn't mean it's not there.'

Gus's whole body seemed to relax. 'I like that.'

A few minutes later, they draped a sheet back over the telescope and turned to leave.

Leo stopped. A chill trickled down his spine. Where was Ralph?

'Are you okay?' Gus's voice sounded as distant as the moon.

Leo mumbled something, but his senses were focused on finding Ralph. He scanned the corners of the room and listened for a rustle in the scraps of material on the floor. Then he caught something move out the window, in Gus's backyard, and the chill left his bones. Ralph was out there, tiptoeing along the top of the fence, a happy shade of gold. He didn't seem interested in the telescope at all.

BACKYARD

That night, Leo rolled two pillows in a blanket. Mum and Dad were in front of the television, so he and Ralph crept down the hallway, away from the lounge room. As he reached for the back door, the television went quiet.

'Where are you going, buddy?'

Ralph held his breath.

Leo had his hand on the doorknob. 'Outside. To look at stars.'

There was a beat of silence. 'By yourself?'

Before Leo could answer, he heard Mum whisper to Dad, 'He's okay. Just let him go.

We need to stop worrying.'

Leo and Ralph ran down the steps. They lay on the blanket, propped up with pillows. Thousands of stars twinkled for their attention.

'Let's make up a new planet,' said Leo. They hadn't played Other Worlds for a while. He didn't know if Ralph would want to.

'Okay.' Ralph stretched his sock feet as far as they could go. 'How about a planet where trees could walk around and live wherever they wanted?'

Leo folded his hands behind his head. 'They could follow the sun when it's cold.'

'Hide behind mountains when it's hot.'

'And the branches would be full of animals who'd go along for the ride.'

They laughed, then lay silent for a while. Leaves rustled and something flapped out of a tree. Leo wanted to talk more, about Gus, or the telescope, or the tower near the lagoon. He opened his mouth, but another voice cut through the night.

'Who are you talking to?'

He sat up. Peg was standing over him, a skinny silhouette in the dark.

'No one.' He felt a kick-drum in his chest.

She sat on the blanket. 'Why do you have two pillows?'

The drum hit harder. 'Because I like two pillows.'

She shrugged, lay back and rested her laced fingers on her belly. 'I was just watching TV with Mum and Dad. It was a show about animals that play tricks. Did you know cuckoos lay their eggs in other birds' nests?'

'I think so.'

'Did you know there's an octopus that changes colour to hide from predators?'

'Really?'

'And did you know that when we were at Gus's place today, your little finger was sticking out the whole time?'

The kick-drum blew apart in his chest. He waited for the sky to crack and the stars to fall down. Ralph froze next to him and blushed a murky purple.

She rolled over. Her face was close to his. 'Is Ralph back?'

Leo took a slow breath. He'd been hiding things for so long. Secret promises, balloon chases, his furry best friend. He was tired of bottling everything up inside, so he told her the truth. 'Yes.'

'Leo!' She grabbed a pillow and swung it at his head. *Thwack!* 'You were supposed to say goodbye!'

'I did but—'

Thwack!

'What happened to making real friends?'

'It's not that easy.'

Thwack!

'But what about Gus?'

He held his hands in front of his face, waiting for the next hit. When it didn't come, he lowered his arms. 'I don't know. I guess he's a friend but . . .' He waited as Ralph scurried back up the stairs and into the house.

They both caught their breath and then Leo went on. 'When I have fun with Gus, Ralph goes somewhere else. Not far, but he leaves us alone. And he's been doing some weird things.'

'Like what?'

'He told me to kick a ball when he knows I can't. And he was busting to see Gus's telescope but when we got there, he didn't even look at it.'

Peg hugged the pillow. 'What's he doing now?'

He nodded towards the house. 'He ran inside.'

Ralph was probably staring at the little clay tower again. Ever since he'd brought it home, Ralph kept looking at it, flapping his golden ears.

Peg shook her head like she was trying to rattle something loose. 'I don't get any of it! You made him up when you were in Prep. Now you're in Year 4. How long is he going to be around? Is he going to stay forever?'

Everything burned inside Leo. Too many thoughts backflipped in his head. He got up and walked around the yard. The dry grass crinkled under his feet and he shooed a fly, still buzzing after dark. Then he came back to the blanket.

'When I met Ralph, he said he'd stay as long as I needed him.'

She pulled a face. 'So? That's just something you made up. Make up another rule.'

'But I think it's true. I don't know why. I just do.'

Why was he spilling it all out? The idea of Ralph had never made sense to Peg. He waited for her to tell him the whole thing was stupid. Or hit him with a pillow.

But she didn't. Instead, she stood up and crossed her arms. 'Do you still need him?'

He heard the question, but he couldn't answer, couldn't even let it in. He imagined it drifting past him like a thread of smoke, curling away into the starry night.

Peg started for the house and then turned back. 'All I know is Gus is really nice and I think you should be friends with him.'

She went inside and Leo was alone on the blanket. He leant back and watched the moon crawl through the sky. He wondered if Gus was watching it too, and it gave him an idea for the pool.

GOAL

The school day hadn't started, and the ground was already hot. Leo could feel it through his shoes as he followed Gus to the middle of the oval.

'What are we doing?'

'I'm going to show you how to kick.'

'Why?'

'Because you don't know how.'

Leo sweated. Everything itched. No wonder Ralph had stayed in the shade. 'But I don't need to know.'

Gus stopped at the chalky halfway line and

trapped the soccer ball under his foot. 'You showed me how to use the telescope. I'm going to show you how to kick a ball.'

Leo scratched his head through his hat. 'Okay.'

'Good,' said Gus. 'Now watch what I do.'

He knelt in the dirt and turned the ball in his hands, like he was trying to find a country on a globe. Satisfied, he placed it on the ground, took a few paces back and stood tall. He locked his eyes on the goal. Took a breath. Then he stepped forward, swung his leg and sent the ball soaring through the air. It sailed a perfect arc and curved into the top corner of the goal.

'Woah.' Leo gulped.

'Your turn.'

Gus collected the ball and positioned it much closer to the goal. Leo stood behind it. Breathed. Then he ran and threw his foot at the ball but missed. Both feet swept off the ground and, for a second, he was in mid-air. Then he fell and hit the dirt.

Gus pulled him up. 'You okay?'

Leo patted the dust off his arms. 'Yeah.'

'At least we don't have to fetch the ball.' Gus slapped him on the back. 'Let's try again.'

This time, Gus slowed everything down for him. Showed him how to measure the steps, where to plant his left foot, and how to swing his right so his laces – not his toe – punched the ball.

'Before you start your run-up, focus on the goal. Look at the exact spot you want the ball to go.'

Leo took off his hat and tossed it out of the way. He measured his steps, sucked a deep breath of air and focused on a tuft of grass sticking up between the goal posts. He stepped up, planted his left foot and swung his right. This time he connected. Felt his laces strike the ball. It bumped along the ground and rebounded off one of the posts. A goofy laugh fell out of his mouth. 'I did it!'

Gus opened his arms. 'Hooray!'

Leo tried a few more kicks. He followed

Gus's tips – focus, step, swing – and got better every time. When it was nearly time for class, Gus carried the ball further from the goal. He teed it up not far from the halfway mark.

'Last one,' he said. 'Try kicking it from here.'

Leo thought he was joking. 'I can't kick that far.'

'Yes, you can.' Gus measured a line between the ball and goal with his eyes. 'My dad said you can always do more than you think.'

Leo readied himself behind the ball. 'I can't do it.'

'Imagine it's something else,' said Gus. 'Something from space. What does it look like?'

That was when Leo remembered. The spaceships from Ralphora were shaped like

giant soccer balls. It would be the last thing he'd see if Ralph ever left: a huge soccer ball rolling up and away from Earth.

He shook the picture from his thoughts and remembered what to do. Stepped forward, swung his foot and thumped the ball into the air. It flew high above the dirt towards the goal.

At the peak of its curve, all he could see was that spinning sphere against the empty sky. His pinky finger twitched and he looked down. Ralph was holding on and watching the ball too.

THE IDEA

A herd of flies followed Leo and Gus to class. Ralph tagged along a few steps behind.

'Did your dad teach you all that soccer stuff?'

Gus dribbled the ball at his feet. 'Yeah.'

'You must miss him a lot.'

'What?' Gus tripped on the ball and nearly fell over. He straightened up, but his face was pale. 'How do you know?'

'Know what? I just meant – because he doesn't live with you.'

Gus was quiet. He picked up the ball and held it tight.

They stopped at the taps, guzzled some water and splashed their faces to cool down.

When they reached the classroom, Leo pulled his pencil case from his bag and a sheet of paper fell out.

Gus picked it up. 'What's this?'

Leo snatched it back. 'Nothing.'

'It said *Ralph*. And there were some big hairy ears.'

'It's just—' Leo looked at the sheet through watery eyes. It was the start of a sketch, just Ralph's ears with his name at the top. 'I was, well, drawing a picture of an alien to, ah, send to Ralph.'

'Oh, okay.' Gus's cheeks reddened and he started to giggle. 'I thought it was, you know, a picture of Ralph. As if he'd look like that.'

Leo faked a laugh and shoved the paper in his bag. He had to talk about something else. 'I've got an idea – to raise money for the pool.'

'Yeah?' Gus tried to balance the ball on his nose. 'What is it?'

The class had moved inside. Ms Pengari was about to mark the roll.

'I want to do something about space. When I showed you how to use the telescope, I thought I could do something like that. Show people what's up in the sky. We could do it on the oval, but it would have to be at night, so I could point out all the things I know. The stars and constellations. The planets we can see. There's so much up there, I reckon people would like it.'

He stopped for a breath. The words were pouring out. He'd never said so many at once and no one had ever listened for that long.

Gus spun the ball in his hands. 'But how would we make money?'

Leo zipped his hat up in his bag. 'Have a barbecue and sell sausages on the night. Hold some sort of raffle. And we could ask for a donation to look through the telescope. It's just – we'd have to use yours. I mean, your dad's. Would that be okay?'

Gus held the ball still. He cleared his throat but didn't say anything. Then he opened his mouth and started to answer, but Ms Pengari poked her head out the door. She wore an eyepatch and a pirate hat and waved a plastic sword.

'Yarrr! What's taking ye so long? We're about to set sail to the land of fractions!'

Both boys started laughing, but Gus stopped first.

'Sorry,' he said. 'But can we talk to you at lunch? Leo's got the best idea to raise money for the pool.'

Leo couldn't shake the grin off his face all morning. Ralph seemed happy too. He practised cartwheels on the carpet and wandered outside to climb trees. He was a warm, hazy gold the whole time.

When lunchtime arrived, Leo and Gus told Ms Pengari the idea. She asked them lots of questions, they scribbled down some details and she told them to think of a name for the event.

Leo tapped his chin. 'What about School Under the Stars?'

Ms Pengari scratched her head with the pirate hook in her hand. 'Could we call it Over the Moon?'

Gus twirled the ball on one finger. He concentrated for a few seconds, then he stopped the ball dead and looked from Leo to the teacher. 'I've got it.' His eyes widened and he said the next bit looking up, as if the words were painted in the sky. 'Dundle After Dark.'

It was perfect.

GONE

There were times when everything felt normal with Ralph, like their morning rides to school. Leo would pedal along the wide Dundle streets while Ralph sat on the handlebars. His furry feet stuck out above the front wheel and if he leant back, he could rest his head in the crook of Leo's neck. Bedtime was just as blissful. They would lay with the sheets pulled up to their chins and watch the stars follow their paths across the sky. Sometimes one of those faraway lights would fizzle and fall and they'd each make a wish. Leo's wish was always the same, to be this happy forever.

At other times, Leo had an off-kilter feeling. Ralph didn't hold his finger as much, he didn't play games and he kept his distance at school, especially when Gus was around. When the two boys practised kicking the ball, Ralph would snooze in a tree. When they chatted in class about Dundle After Dark, Ralph rolled somersaults at the other end of the room. Leo wanted to keep both friends. He didn't want one to erase the other. But he couldn't tell Gus any more about Ralph, not after he'd laughed at his unfinished drawing.

Then one day his furry friend slipped from view and Leo didn't know where he was.

It happened on a Saturday when Gus was at Leo's house. They spent the morning working on Dundle After Dark, writing lists, drawing ideas and planning space-themed activities.

'There was a silly game I used to play with Ralph,' said Leo. 'All we did was bounce a balloon and stop it from touching the ground.'

Gus pulled a face. 'Everyone's done that.'

'I know that now, but when I was five, I thought I'd invented it. We gave it a really bad name too.'

Gus held out his hands. 'What was it?'

'Bounce the Moon!'

They both fell into a fit of giggles.

'That's terrible!' Gus shook his head and smiled.

Leo sighed and rubbed his eyes. Then he spotted Ralph sitting on the floor in the next room. His fur was watery blue.

As they worked at the dining table, Leo's parents joined in. Dad sketched a map of the event and Mum helped them write out the steps for the games.

'This is going to be so much fun,' she said. 'You boys have done a great job.'

When they were done, they played a card game with Peg.

'Ralph never plays cards with me,' she whispered to Leo.

Then they played Bounce the Moon, but they kept laughing and falling over.

After the game, they lay under the fan in the lounge room. Gus held the balloon and asked about Ralph. 'Did he know lots of space stuff like you?'

'Yeah. Heaps more.'

'And how long were you friends?'

'Ever since Prep.'

Gus turned the balloon in his hands, the way he sometimes did with his soccer ball. 'What did he look like?'

Leo's heart beat twice as fast, but he tried to keep his voice normal. 'What do you mean?'

'I don't know. Was he tall or short? Did he have big ears or anything?'

'Um.' Leo rocked up and sat crosslegged. What did Gus know? He looked around for his furry friend, but he wasn't in the lounge room. He jumped to his feet and ran to his room. It was empty. Gus called out, but Leo didn't listen. He ran to every room. Flung the doors open and dropped to the floor to search under furniture. He checked the verandah, the backyard and under the house. Ralph was gone.

Leo was sitting on the front fence when Gus walked down the steps and found him.

'What happened? Are you okay?'

Leo gripped the cold steel of the fence. He had to hold on tight because he thought the whole planet might crumble around him. 'Yeah. No. Not really.'

'I didn't mean to say anything wrong. I was just asking—'

'Forget it.' Leo faced his friend. He could never tell the truth about Ralph, that he was an alien with flappy ears that no one else could see. Instead, he tightened his grip. 'You should probably just go home.'

Gus picked up his bike and rode away, holding the ball under one arm. Leo stayed on the fence for the rest of the afternoon. The world didn't collapse, like he thought it might. But he didn't see Ralph and that felt just as bad.

TRUTH

The moon was a crescent, a thin fingernail in the sky. Leo watched it from the verandah in his pyjamas and, even though it wasn't cold, he hugged his knees to his chest. He replayed the afternoon in his head and then he tried to forget it. The slice of moon slowly disappeared. For a second, he didn't know why. It had been so long since he'd seen a cloud.

Mum came out to the verandah and sat beside him. She had checked on him a few times when he'd planted himself on the fence. Watched him at dinner without saying a word.

Now she followed his gaze to the Dundle sky as the skinny moon reappeared.

'I remember when you were five,' she said. 'You'd ask me all those questions about space. I told you as much as I could but pretty soon, you knew more than me.'

He didn't move or say anything. Didn't know what he wanted to do.

'Leo.' Her voice was light, like a balloon, but he knew something heavy was hanging on. 'I know about Ralph. I know he came back.'

He held his legs tighter. 'Did Peg tell you?'

'She didn't have to, love. I knew he was here.'

Leo's body was coiled tight, every muscle tense. He had spent all this time hiding things, bottling up secrets and bending the truth. It was all for nothing. Peg had worked out that Ralph was around. Mum and Dad had probably known all along. They knew his secret and he had nothing left to keep locked inside, so he let go of his legs, dropped his arms by his sides and breathed out slowly, like air escaping a pinhole in a soccer ball. As his breath stretched out and away, he imagined his secrets spilling and dissolving into the sky. He felt lighter than he had for a long time. His body was loose and unwound.

'Are you mad?'

She shook her head. 'A bit disappointed, but that's okay. I thought he might come back. But I'm worried about what happened this afternoon. It was something to do with Ralph, wasn't it?'

He nodded and told her that Ralph was gone. He shivered when he said it out loud. His heart was empty of the secrets he'd let go, but it left behind a blank space, a hole in the shape of Ralph.

Neither of them spoke for a minute. A possum skittered along a powerline. A night bird called through the dark.

Mum reached and held his hand, the same way she had done the first time he told her about Ralph. 'I don't know where he's gone, but he wouldn't leave forever without saying goodbye.'

'I think I upset him today,' he said. 'Because I made fun of our old games.'

Mum moved closer. 'Whatever happens with your imaginary friend, don't lose the real-life one you've made.'

He shrank in his chair. He felt awful about sending Gus home.

'You've done so well. Gus is becoming a good friend. And I know it means a lot to him, after all that he's been through.'

'You mean his dad?'

'Yeah.' She squeezed his hand. 'Must be hard for him.'

He got out of his chair and paced along the verandah. Thought of all the things he and Gus had done in just a few weeks. They had shared Gus's telescope, played soccer and planned Dundle After Dark. Mum was right. Gus was a good friend.

He turned to her. 'What should I do?'

She stood up and gave him a one-armed hug. 'Secrets between friends only get in the way. So tell him the truth. You know – the one with flappy ears.'

SORRY

Mum was right. Ralph hadn't gone forever. He tiptoed into Leo's room before he fell asleep.

'Ralph?' Leo blinked in the dark.

His friend slipped into bed and wrapped his hairy sock paws around him. 'I'm sorry.'

Leo yawned. 'Where have you been all day?'

'Promise you won't get mad?'

'I promise.'

Ralph puffed a heavy breath. 'I climbed to the top of the tower.'

Leo rolled over to face him. 'What was it like?'

‘Beautiful.’ His eyes twinkled as he described the world from up high: the land rolling away like a dark ocean, the sky awash with stars, and the tiny orange lights peeking out from all the houses.

‘I waited for you all day,’ said Leo. ‘I was worried you wouldn’t come back.’

Ralph wiggled his nose. ‘I was always coming back. I hadn’t said goodbye.’

‘Will you disappear like that again?’

He twitched his horns and flapped an ear. ‘I’ll be here as long as you need me.’

Leo closed his eyes. It didn’t sound like forever anymore. It didn’t sound long at all.

PINKY FINGER

A few days later, Dundle woke to its hottest morning of the year. The stove-top heat pressed in from all sides. Leo sweated the whole day, wilting at his desk like a thirsty plant. Ms Pengari sprayed misty water on the children's faces. She wore a pair of pilot's goggles strapped to her head – they were supposed to be flying to the twin islands of Area and Perimeter, but everyone was too hot and tired.

'It's days like these we need that pool more than ever,' she said. 'The sooner we raise some money, the sooner we can go for a swim.'

Nicola, the girl with the horse, raised her hand. 'Do you think it'll really happen? How much money do we need?'

Ms Pengari sprayed water on her own face before she answered. 'I spoke to someone at the council. They said ten thousand dollars would be a good start.'

The class erupted into gasps and howls.

'That's way too much!' one boy called out.

'Yeah,' said another. 'That's like a million bucks!'

The gasps turned to laughter before Ms Pengari calmed them down.

'You all have such good ideas for raising money. I think we'll get close. And the first fundraiser is at the end of next week, Dundle After Dark. Leo and Gus – is everything on track?'

Leo gave something between a nod and a shrug and glanced across the room at Gus. They hadn't talked since Leo had told him to go home.

Ms Pengari didn't ask any more questions, but she caught Leo before he went to morning tea. 'Should I be worried about Dundle After Dark? Or more worried about you and Gus?'

Leo stretched his finger and Ralph grabbed on. 'We planned everything at my place on Saturday. But something happened and we haven't talked again.'

She pulled the goggles from her forehead. 'Are you going to try talking today?'

He shifted from foot to foot. 'Mum said I should. That I need to tell him the truth.'

'The truth?' she said. 'About Ralph?'

He squinted at his teacher. 'How much do you know about Ralph?'

She polished her goggles with a tissue. 'Oh, you mean the little guy holding onto your finger right now?'

Leo's eyes popped. He looked at his honey-coloured friend, then shook his head and laughed. 'I'm really bad at hiding him.'

'I wouldn't say that. Your parents told me to

keep an eye on that finger. And I don't think *every*one knows about him – are you worried about telling Gus?'

He nodded, head down.

'Remember I said you needed to find someone who likes the way you don't fit? That someone is Gus. He already likes that you're different. And having a Ralph makes you fit even less, so I think he'll like you more.'

It was all a bit confusing.

'Okay,' he said. 'Thanks.'

She sprayed him with water and shooed him out the door.

THE DRAWING

For the rest of the morning, two voices overlapped in Leo's head – his mum's and Ms Pengari's. He had to share his secret and he got his chance at lunchtime.

He found Gus in the shady spot next to the library.

'Hey,' he said. 'Is it okay if I sit down?'

Gus moved his lunchbox to make room.

'I'm really sorry,' Leo said. 'I wrecked the whole day when I told you to go.'

The soccer ball was between them. Gus picked it up and turned it around. 'Felt like I wrecked it when I talked about Ralph. But I don't know why.'

Leo felt a squeeze on his finger.

Ralph was right there. He blinked his glassy eyes, and his fur was sunnier than ever. 'Go on,' he said in his soft growly voice. 'Tell him.'

Leo had brought an exercise book from his desk. He opened it to a fresh page and fished a lead pencil out of his pocket.

'There are some things I haven't told you,' he said. 'About Ralph.'

The thump and shout of a footy game echoed across the school as Leo started to draw.

'He's a bit shorter than me,' he said. 'About a metre tall. And he's all furry, like this.'

He scribbled a hairy lump in the shape of Ralph's body. Gus leant over the page, hardly blinking. Ralph sat close with a paw on Leo's shoulder.

'He's got these pointy hands and feet, a bit like scruffy socks.' He added them to the page. 'And stubby horns on top.'

'Horns?' said Gus.

'Yeah. They wiggle around.'

Ralph stroked the little stumps on his head.

Leo kept drawing, describing each part of his friend as it appeared. The bulgy black nose, the long flappy ears and those sparkly eyes. When the sketch was done, he sat back and looked from the picture to Gus, wondering if this was a good idea. He had opened the cage that held his secret, and he didn't know what came next. On the hottest day of his life, he suddenly felt cold. Ralph's fur cooled to an icy grey.

Gus picked up the book. 'This is Ralph? With those big ears?'

Leo nodded and that old jellyfish woke up in his belly.

'And he's … an alien?'

Another nod. The jellyfish stirred.

'So Ralph is—'

Leo finished the thought. 'My imaginary friend.'

Gus didn't take his eyes off the page. His

eyebrows squashed together. He must have been wrestling with his own memories, leafing back through their conversations. Then his face brightened up and he looked at Leo. 'He looks so friendly. Did you really make him up?'

A breath eased from Leo's chest and the jellyfish settled again.

'I thought you'd laugh. Like you laughed at that picture I hadn't finished.'

Gus shook his head. 'Sorry … I didn't mean—' He smiled again at the drawing. 'I just didn't expect it. I've never had an imaginary friend. What's it like?'

For the next few minutes, Leo told Gus everything about Ralph: the day their friendship started, all the games they'd played, the telescope, the great pig chase and the night they said goodbye. Then he talked about Saturday, when Ralph had disappeared to the tower and Leo sulked on the fence.

'I'm sorry,' he said. 'It was stupid.'

'Doesn't matter.' Gus twirled the ball on his

finger, but it wobbled and fell to the ground. 'Wait—' His eyes searched around Leo. 'Is he here now?'

'Sitting next to me.'

Gus stared at the space beside Leo. Ralph was there, smiling, but to Gus, it must have been just a patch of empty pavers. 'I wish I could see him,' he said. 'He sounds like the best friend in the world.'

'Yeah. He is.'

Ralph's fur washed gold and Leo felt the same. He had shared his biggest truth and now another had emerged – that there was more than one best friend in the world: real-life Gus, a boy twice his size, who could kick a soccer ball as high as the moon; and Ralph, his flappy-eared alien that no one else could see. Leo looked at his furry friend, huddled beside him, and remembered what he had said. *I'll be here as long as you need me.*

OLD GAMES

In the days leading up to Dundle After Dark, everyone helped Leo and Gus get ready. Dad collected the sausages for the barbecue. Mum borrowed boxes of lanterns and lights from her boss, Mr Oliver. Gus's mum polished the telescope and cleaned the eyepiece and lens. The boys stuck up posters, printed out programs and put messages in the school newsletter.

When no one else was around, Ralph wanted to play their old games again. They bounced the moon around Leo's room, hunted for asteroids in the garden, and stomped through an obstacle course in the yard, pretending they were somewhere in space. The friends threw themselves into the games and tumbled in laughter. At night, they lay on the blanket and played Other Worlds. They didn't invent new planets or aliens but talked about their old favourites. The species that looked like doughnuts. The planet of tiny elephants. Ralphora and its fairy-floss trees and lemonade rivers.

The night before Dundle After Dark, they sat on the verandah. Trees rustled with nighttime creatures and a newsreader droned on from a television across the road.

'I can't wait for tomorrow,' said Leo.

'Me too.' Ralph stared straight ahead. Jupiter shone bright and he couldn't take his eyes off it. 'Leo – before you moved to Dundle, you wanted to see a spaceship. Do you still think about that?'

'Sometimes.' Leo raised an eyebrow. 'Why?'

His friend didn't answer. They sat a while longer, padded off to bed and said their backwards goodbye.

'Tomorrow you see.'

'Tomorrow you see.'

GUS'S STORY

Leo didn't go home after school the next day. His bike stayed in the racks while he and Gus set up the lights for Dundle After Dark. They hung a pair of camping lanterns at the front gate, planted a trail of small garden lamps near the oval, and made an arrow of tealights that would lead to the telescope. Last of all, they wound fairy lights around tree trunks and hung a string of coloured bulbs outside the toilets.

Most of the class had stayed back to get things ready. They decorated moon cakes and hammered signs into the ground. When Leo and Gus finished their jobs, they sat on the double slide in the junior playground, waiting for the sun to fall and for families to arrive.

'Where's Ralph now?'

Leo pointed. 'Over there.'

Ralph rocked on one of the swings. He watched the sky without blinking.

'Thanks for telling me about him.' Gus lay back on the slide and used his soccer ball as a pillow. 'There's something I've kept a secret too. It's about my dad.'

Leo lay on the next-door slide and waited.

Gus huffed a breath. 'I said I haven't seen him for ages and, well …' His voice wavered. 'I won't ever see him again.'

Leo's body was pinned down by the sky, but he turned to face Gus. 'You mean …?'

He couldn't say it. He didn't need to.

'It's been nearly two years,' said Gus. 'I keep thinking he's gonna be there when I get home from school, but he never is.'

The night was silent. Even the birds and

cicadas held their voices. Leo was quiet too, but he edged one sentence into the dark. 'That ball's pretty special, hey.'

'Yeah.'

That's all they said for a while. Leo didn't mind. It was Gus's story to tell and maybe that was all he wanted to say.

Gus rested his hands on his chest. 'What was that thing you said about the moon, when you can't see it in the sky?'

Leo remembered. It was the same thing his dad had said about the universe, years ago. 'Just because you can't see something, doesn't mean it's not there.'

'That's it.' Gus laughed. For such a big kid, it came out like a soft breath. 'I think about that all the time. I can't see Dad anymore, but I think he's still here, or up there.' He pointed at the almost-full moon.

DUNDLE AFTER DARK

At last, the light gave way to dark, and another clear night sky stretched over the town. Car headlights rounded the corner and families started to drift through the gate. Gus's mum and grandma arrived, and the boys carried the telescope to the centre of the oval. More people stepped out of cars, parents and grandparents and kids in pyjamas. The covered area was full of excited voices. One of the kids started some music that pumped out of a big speaker.

Leo's family turned up and Mum gave him a hug.

‘There are so many people!’ said Peg.

Dad squeezed Leo’s shoulder. ‘Great job, buddy.’

Families chatted to each other. Teachers were mingling too. After a while, the music stopped and everyone turned to Ms Pengari, standing on a bench seat and holding a microphone. She wore a puffy orange astronaut suit, with a space helmet under her arm.

‘Welcome to Dundle After Dark!’

The crowd cheered. Leo’s body tingled and Ralph gripped his finger.

‘Thank you, everyone. It’s going to be a very special night.’

Ralph held on a bit tighter.

‘We are hoping to raise lots of money to reopen the town pool. I’m not going to say much more because I’ll hand you over to Leo and Gus.’

Everyone clapped as the boys made their way to the front.

Gus took the microphone from Ms Pengari

but handed it straight to Leo. 'It's your idea,' he said.

Leo trembled as he started to talk. 'Um, thank you for, ah, coming.' His words hobbled out of his mouth. He lowered the microphone and whispered to Gus. 'I can't do it. Can you talk instead?'

Gus bounced the ball in his hands. 'Okay.' He took the microphone. 'Tonight is all about space. There are games to play, over there.' He pointed to a space near the office, where Moon Walk was set up. 'There's a big raffle, with lots of prizes. And later on, there'll be sausages and soft drinks for sale. But the best thing we have is the telescope on the oval. For a small donation, I'll show you how to use it, and Leo will tell you about all the things in the sky. The moon is out, and Leo said we'll see Jupiter and Venus. There are lots of constellations too.'

He leant close to Leo. 'Anything else? Do you want to say something?'

Leo looked from Gus to the crowd and back.

'You can do it,' said Gus. 'Like my dad said – you can always do more than you think.'

Leo took the microphone. He scanned the crowd for the faces he knew. Mum, Dad and Peg, all of them beaming. Ralph, halfway up a post, giving a small wave. And Gus beside him, his real-life friend, telling him he could do it.

He puffed out his chest. 'Thanks for coming, everyone. It's gonna be fun. And who knows – we might even see a UFO.'

The crowd laughed and then clapped again, as loud as a rocket taking off. Leo had never talked in front of so many people. He and Gus led everyone along the candlelit path, all the way to the telescope. Gus had been practising at home, so he looked like an expert as he twisted knobs and angled the tube. Then he invited people to look through the eyepiece, showing them how to focus the lens. As they did, Leo pointed out the wonders of the world above. The craters on the moon. The nearest planets.

The shape of constellations, those dot-to-dot pictures made of stars.

The buddies from his first week at school were there, and Nicola, the girl with the horse, kept asking questions.

'What's that? Just above the trees?'

'Venus,' said Leo.

'What about those stars?' She pointed higher in the sky.

'That's Scorpius. Looks a bit like a scorpion.'

'Is there—' She rocked back and stared. 'Is there a horse up there?'

Her eyes were wide and her mouth was open, like she had never seen a night sky before. As Leo started to answer, Ralph grabbed his finger, but he shook him off so he could finish talking. 'Sort of. There's a constellation called Pegasus. But we can't see it, not till later in the year.'

'Really? Wow.'

As he shared his love of the sky with more people, an old feeling rose up inside. That big balloon feeling, like his chest was filled with air – but now he'd given it to others too. Kids and parents were gazing up, whispering and pointing at the patterns above. On that dusty oval under the dark Dundle sky, he felt like he was a part of a constellation himself – a cluster of people, marvelling at space, and joined together with invisible lines.

The Earth turned slowly, the moon rose higher and after a while, everyone had peered through the telescope at the star-filled sky. The smell of sausages wafted across the oval and families flocked to the barbecue.

'Come on, Leo.' Gus was waiting for him to follow the crowd to the food. Nicola was waiting too, and a few other kids.

Ralph tugged his finger again. Without looking down, he whispered to his friend. 'Later, Ralph. I'm hungry.'

He caught up to Gus and the others and they ran to the covered area. Everyone was chatting, kids were playing Moon Walk, and Leo grabbed a sausage from Dad.

‘Well done, bud. Look at all these faces. Listen to the noise!’

It was a strange sound. There must have been a hundred people talking at once. Leo couldn’t make out what anyone was saying, but their voices swam together to make one big instrument, happy and loud.

When he had finished eating, he followed the tealights back to the telescope and stood on the oval by himself. Quiet there in the middle, away from all the chatter and music. He rested his hand on the scope, then peeked through the eyepiece. Spent some time with the almost-full moon, named in his head all the lunar seas, then he panned across to find a constellation. But along the way he spotted something strange. A small bright dot but bigger than a star. He kept the scope still, watching the dot – it was moving, travelling slowly across the sky, growing as it went. He followed its path, keeping it in sight. It wasn’t just flying, it seemed to be rolling. A big round shape, spinning through the night.

'Oh no.'

He took his eye from the telescope and looked up. He could see it, moving among the stars. He knew what it was, where it had come from and why it was getting bigger.

He sprinted across the oval, straight to the bike racks. He jumped on his bike, hit the pedals and skidded out the gate. As he sped along the road, he kept his eyes on the sky. There was a soccer ball spaceship heading towards Dundle and he didn't have much time.

THE TOP OF THE TOWER

There weren't many streetlights in Dundle. The wide empty streets were dark, the houses and trees still. Leo pushed the pedals and tracked the ball in the sky as he rode. The only sounds were the tyres whirring along and his breathing, heavy and hard.

He rode past his house, over the train tracks and down the main street. There were streetlights here and light falling from the pubs, but no one would have noticed him streaking past or the spaceship high above. It was still a distant ball but getting closer, whirling through the dark. He reached the lagoon and kept going, over a bumpy wooden bridge to the other side. Then he stopped. The black shape of the tower loomed over him. In the dark, it looked like an enormous upturned rocket that had nosedived towards the ground, but got caught by the tangle of timber legs. He traced with his eyes the steps that zigzagged through the heart of the wooden frame. It was a long way up.

He scrabbled over the fence and landed heavily. He caught his breath and pressed his hand on one of the giant wooden legs. It was hard and rough. He scooted up the steps, his shoes thudding on the timber. When he reached the top, he was puffed again. He bent over with his hands on his knees. Waited for his head to stop spinning.

'Leo?'

A warm growly voice came from the other side of the tower.

'Ralph!' He staggered around and hugged his friend. 'You didn't say goodbye.'

Ralph patted his back. 'I'm still here. And I knew you'd come.' He pulled out of the hug and swept his paw towards the view. 'Look at this planet of yours.'

From that height, above the tops of the trees, the world was beautiful. In every direction, the land unrolled like thick rumpled carpet in the dark. A cluster of warm lights glinted from the town: bedroom lamps and TV screens, keeping people company. Up above, the navy sky was dusted with stars and the soccer ball spaceship was bigger again, about the size of the moon.

'Is it really coming for you?'

Ralph nodded.

'So that means—'

He couldn't finish, so Ralph spoke for him.

'It's time to say goodbye.' The words caught in his throat and the sparkly light of the moon gleamed in his eyes.

Leo sat on the balcony, holding his knees. 'You're supposed to stay as long as I need you.'

Ralph kept facing the sky. 'I know.'

'But—'

'Listen.' Ralph rested his paws on Leo's shoulders. When he spoke again, his voice was husky. He sounded tired. 'I came from Ralphora because you needed a friend. And you've been the best friend in the universe. But you don't need me anymore.'

'I do!'

'No.' Ralph slowed his voice down. 'You don't. Not anymore. You needed a friend and you've got one. But it's not me. It's Gus.'

Leo wanted to scream at Ralph and tell him he was wrong. But he knew, deep down, everything his friend had said was true. All Ralph's thoughts and all his words, tonight and last week and all the days before, had come from the same place. They had come from Leo.

When Ralph pestered Leo to say hi to Gus, it was Leo who wanted him to stop and sit down. When Ralph had told him to kick the ball, it was really Leo's wish. When Ralph had gazed at the strange tower, it was Leo who decided that one night they would climb it, the night they would say goodbye. In the deepest pocket of his heart, Leo knew all along that this moment would come, because he had designed it himself. They had played their old games, imagined their planets and, the night before, said their final Grimble farewells.

Now here they were, on top of the tower, watching the spaceship descend. There wasn't much time and Leo wanted to imagine Ralph longer, to hear his voice in his head a bit more.

'Where will you go after this?'

Ralph wiggled a horn. 'Back to Ralphora.'

'Will you help someone else one day?'

'Of course. That's what Ralphs do.'

Leo held Ralph in his eyes. He didn't want to let go. 'I'm going to miss you.'

'I'll miss you too.' Ralph took Leo's hand in his paw. 'But just because you can't see something, doesn't mean it's not there.'

It happened quickly in the end. It was better that way. The two friends hugged on the roof. Ralph's fur was as soft as ever and it glittered in the starlight. They held on for a minute before Leo finally let go. The spaceship eased down and hovered over the tower. It was the size of a small building, and it hardly made a sound – just a quiet hum, like a fridge at night.

From the bottom of the ship, a hatch opened and out floated a white balloon. It drifted straight down until its ribbon dangled next to Ralph. He flapped his ears and twitched his nose, then flung himself into Leo's arms one last time. He broke off, blinked his sparkly eyes and grabbed the ribbon. He gave a final wave, and the balloon lifted him into the ship. The last thing Leo saw was Ralph's furry foot before the hatch closed. It was the colour of a golden sunrise.

STAIRCASE TO THE STARS

Leo was alone. He stared at the shrinking spaceship until it was a speck. The moon and stars moved further on their course, then he lay on the balcony and closed his eyes. He thought of Ralph and his sunshine fur, his gravelly voice and watery eyes. At that moment, he didn't miss his friend. He had stayed as long as he needed to stay and helped as much as he could. Leo had needed a friend and Ralph had opened his eyes to Gus.

He would miss Ralph, but he didn't feel sad. He was happy to have imagined him at all.

A breeze feathered his face, waking a cold thought in his head. The last time he had seen Gus – or anyone else – was back at school, at Dundle After Dark. He had run away from the whole thing and now they'd all be looking for him. Mum, Dad and Peg. Maybe Ms Pengari and the other kids. They'd be searching the school, or calling the police, and no one would know he was on top of the tower.

He'd be in trouble when they found him. The whole world would start worrying again. He could climb down now and find them first, or stay at the top, hiding.

His head started to itch. His heart beat faster. The jellyfish threatened to wake in his belly. Then he heard something. Footsteps, coming up the tower. They were soft at first, just one pair of feet. He waited, huddled, as the footsteps grew louder. Then someone appeared. A big kid with a soccer ball under his arm.

'Leo? Are you okay?'

Leo stood up. 'Hey. I'm, look, sorry I—'

There was the sound of more feet, clunking up the timber steps, louder and louder, nearing the top. They burst onto the balcony. Mum first, then Dad and Peg.

'Leo!' cried Mum.

They rushed and threw their arms around him.

'I'm sorry.'

'We didn't know where you were,' she said. 'But – oh, wow.'

She leant on the railing, taking in the view. The others joined her, quiet, in slow motion. The sky was like a star-spattered sheet above them, the land a midnight sea.

'Look.' Gus nodded towards the town. 'You can see school from here.'

Leo traced the path of house lights all the way to the school. The cars were still there. It was too far to see them but all those people, that hundred-voice choir, were still talking and laughing and pointing at the sky, all because of him.

He pushed his voice into the dark. 'How did

you know where I was?'

The family shared a look. 'None of us had a clue,' said Dad. 'It was Gus who thought you might have come here.' He patted Gus on the back. 'You've got a great friend here, Leo. He knows you better than any of us.'

Gus grinned and tossed the ball from hand to hand.

Mum and Dad didn't ask many questions. They said they'd save it for home.

'This is incredible,' said Mum. 'Like we're halfway between the Earth and space.'

Dad spun round. 'It's a staircase to the stars.'

Peg shot a finger in the air. 'I know why Leo came here – it's a lookout – for UFOs!'

To Leo, it was all those things but, more than that, it was a place to say goodbye.

On the way down, Peg whispered to Leo. 'What happened tonight? Was it something with Ralph?'

He cupped his answer behind his hand. 'He's gone.'

She kinked her eyebrows. 'You don't need him anymore?'

'Nope.'

She hugged him again.

At the bottom of the tower, he waited for Gus and they climbed back over the fence.

He picked up his bike. 'Sorry I left Dundle After Dark.'

'It's still going, you know. No one wants to go home.'

'Good – I want to look through the telescope again.'

Gus bounced the ball. Leo wheeled his bike.

'And thanks,' said Leo. 'For finding me.'

He was talking about much more than tonight, and he could tell Gus knew what he meant. Mum and Dad let them walk back in the dark. Leo pushed his bike and Gus twirled his ball. On the way, Leo told him all about his last moments with Ralph. The white balloon, his shimmery fur and the soccer ball sailing away.

THE NAME

Days later, Mum tapped on Leo's bedroom door.

'Hey, love.'

'Hi.'

Leo was at his desk, reading a book from the school library. It was called *Stargazing in the Southern Sky*. He was learning more constellations to spot with Gus's telescope.

Mum sat on the bed. 'Tell me something from the book.'

He dragged his finger along a page. 'This is one of my favourites – it's called a Jewel Box cluster.'

'That sounds pretty.'

'Yeah, it is.' He read from the book. 'It looks like a few bright stars, but through a telescope, there's about a hundred. All red and blue.'

'I'd love to see that.' She held her hands together. 'You going okay?'

He bookmarked the page and closed the book. Then turned to her. 'Yeah.' He swung his legs. 'I don't need him back, but I still miss him.'

She smiled. 'I'm proud of you. Moving here. Making friends with Gus. Saying goodbye to Ralph – again.'

Leo spun a circle in his chair. 'Can I ask you something?'

'What is it?'

'Leo!' Peg yelled from somewhere in the house. 'Gus is here!'

He stopped spinning and looked at the hallway, then back at Mum. 'I was wondering – why did you call him Ralph?'

She blinked a few times. 'Me? What do you mean?'

'You were the one who named him Ralph. Where did you get the name?'

She faced the window. The sunlight coloured her face. 'I just always liked it. I had a friend called Ralph.'

'Really?'

'When I was a kid. I was bit like you, you know.'

Leo jumped from his chair to the bed. 'Wait a minute – what kind of friend?'

'Leo!' It was Peg again. 'Gus is waiting!'

Mum smiled at him and held the side of his face in her hand. 'A story for another day. You'd better go and say hi to Gus.'

He backed off the bed. Stared at her until he got to the hallway. Then he ran out to meet Gus, who was waiting at the front door with his ball. They said a quick hi, then stomped down the steps and jumped the fence into the high school. For the rest of the afternoon, they played on the patchy soccer field. They practised their passes, shot for goal and sent the ball flying through the sky.

EPILOGUE

Leo and Gus walked through the gates with towels over their shoulders. It was a steamy Saturday morning and half the town was at the pool, like a flock of birds crowding a dam.

'This is it!' Gus opened his arms wide. 'That's the main pool there. Deep end is that way and this is the shallow end here. The kiddies' pool is over there – there's a plastic slide, but I'm too big for it. I'm gonna jump in the deep end. What do you want to do?'

Leo scanned the pool. The shallow end was packed with kids, splashing and jumping and tumbling round. Someone waved from the crowd.

'Is that Nicola?'

Gus squinted. 'Yeah. And Rafi. And Mia.'

The boys ran to the pool.

Nicola tumble-turned under the water, then lifted herself onto the edge. 'Hey!'

'Hi.' Drops of water landed on Leo's feet. He couldn't wait to jump in. 'We're going to the deep end.'

'Okay!' She climbed out, followed them, then turned and called to Rafi and Mia. 'Come on – deep end!'

They lined up behind a diving block, but Leo hung back. He pulled his polaroid camera from his backpack. It still worked after all this time.

'Dive in and I'll take your picture.'

Rafi went first, a perfect dolphin dive, like a sword piercing the surface. Leo snapped a photo and the camera printed it out. Mia was next – a star-jump crash – and he took another photo. Then Nicola's pencil dive, straight and thin. And finally Gus, who sprang off the block, hugged his knees, and plummeted into the pool like a boulder thrown from the sky.

Leo piled the photos together and tucked them in a pocket of his bag.

Gus called from the edge. 'What are you gonna do with the pictures?'

'I've got an album at home,' he said. 'I'll stick them in.'

He kicked off his shoes, lumped them together with his towel and stood on the diving block. The blazing sun hit his back for a few more seconds, then he leapt in. The water cooled his bones and cleaned him of the prickly heat. He swam along the bottom, under the lane ropes, until he reached the other side. When he popped up through the surface, Gus was right there beside him.

'This is so good,' Leo said.

'I know!' Gus dived under and held a handstand.

Leo floated on his back, squinting at the sky. It had been spotless blue since the day he arrived, but now it was changing colour. The blue gave way to a whitish haze. Dark grey leaked at the edges. Children stopped swimming and looked up, as a carpet of clouds spread over the town. The first drops stuttered, light and unsure, then the rain rushed down in sheets. Children squealed, the grown-ups cheered, and it felt like Dundle could breathe again.

Leo kept floating on the surface of the pool. The rain hit his face, his arms and his chest. He closed his eyes and thought of the world above the rain, beyond the clouds, further than he could see. Somewhere out there, the moon Ralphora followed its course, performing an endless loop. And on the moon would be Ralph, dipping his head in the lemonade river or trotting around with the other Ralphs. Maybe he'd already left his home and had found a new friend who needed his help.

They swam in the rain until their fingers were wrinkled and soft. When the pool finally closed for the day, Leo and Gus said goodbye to the others and started riding home. The rain fell lightly, and steam rose from the wet bitumen. The brown yards were soaked. Stormwater drains gurgled. The whole town seemed to sparkle.

The boys didn't talk as they rode, not until they reached the turn where Gus went one way and Leo went the other.

As they pedalled away from each other, Gus called over his shoulder. 'Tomorrow you see.'

Leo waved. 'Tomorrow you see.'

Then he rode home in the rain and nothing could wash the smile from his face.

ACKNOWLEDGEMENTS

I love writing stories, but I always find it hard. As I wrote this book, some generous and talented people encouraged, supported and challenged me to make *Leo and Ralph* shine brighter than I thought possible. It was still hard, but they made it much easier. Thank you to the following:

Clair Hume, for helping me find the story in the idea.

Cathy Vallance, for sharpening the text and illustrations on every level.

Mark Macleod, for an edit that strengthened the story and taught me so much, again.

Thanks also to Jo Hunt for a sparkling cover design, and Kate Garaty for making the internals shine.

To the whole UQP team, thank you for working together to launch another book into the world for me.

Thank you to all the bookshops, libraries, teachers, librarians and parents who put books in the hands of children.

Finally, thanks to my family, especially Bron, Sophie and Willow (my unofficial story supervisor) for being there for me, as I sat in the corner of the house, dreaming all of this up.